PRAIRIE VENGEANCE

Wayne C. Lee

Chivers Press • G.K. Hall & Co.
Bath, England • Thorndike, Maine USA

This Large Print edition is published by Chivers Press, England, and by G.K. Hall & Co., USA.

Published in 1998 in the U.K. by arrangement with Golden West Literary Agency.

Published in 1998 in the U.S. by arrangement with Golden West Literary Agency.

U.K. Hardcover ISBN 0-7540-3193-4 (Chivers Large Print)
U.K. Softcover   ISBN 0-7540-3194-2 (Camden Large Print)
U.S. Softcover   ISBN 0-7838-8379-X (Nightingale Series Edition)

The text of this Large Print edition is unabridged.
Other aspects of the book may vary from the original edition.

Set in 16 pt. New Times Roman.

Printed in Great Britain on acid-free paper.

British Library Cataloguing in Publication Data available

Library of Congress Cataloging-in-Publication Data

Lee, Wayne C.
      Prairie vengeance / by Wayne C. Lee.
            p.   cm.
      ISBN 0-7838-8379-X (lg. print : sc : alk. paper)
      1. Large type books.   I. Title.
      [PS3523.E34457P73   1998]

      813' .54-dc21   97-44867

Jim Taylor had signed up to work on Claude Verdune's Flying V Bar spread, and was on his way there when he stopped to chat with the members of Wes Ward's nester caravan. Thus it was that he found himself in the thick of a six-gun attack on the wagons, and soon was forced to take sides against Verdune in spite of himself.So instead of going to the Flying V Bar, Jim set up shop in the new and booming town of Bluestem, which was also controlled by Verdune. Although everyone from the local newspaper editor to the grocery store owner was cowed by Verdune, they resented his domination and were only too eager to find a man willing to fight him. And Jim, with his gumption and dogged courage, seemed like the logical man.

A hard-hitting yarn of the Nebraska plains in the days when the very mention of the word 'homesteader' sent ranchers' hands to their gun-belts.

CHAPTER ONE

Jim Taylor kicked a chip into the fire and looked at the little group around him. He had seen homesteaders before, whole caravans of them, but never any quite like this.

There was Wes Ward, a little man, the leader of the wagon train, but leader in name only, Jim guessed. And Gramp Shepherd, still smaller than Ward but with twice the backbone and four times the drive, if Jim was any judge of men.

He turned to look at the girl, Betty Ward. No man was liable to forget her once he had seen her. Tall and straight, with smooth even features and two long braids of brown hair that managed to sparkle even in the flickering light of the fire. And her deep brown eyes would make a man fight his head when she looked at him.

There were others, but they had gone to their wagons for the night. For the most part they were ordinary settlers. But Jim saw fire in Gramp Shepherd that was reflected in all the others except Wes Ward. It seemed to Jim that there wasn't anything inside Ward to make a reflection. But the unusual determination that burned in these home seekers brought a worried frown to Jim's brow.

'You're sure your locations are several miles

1

upstream?' he asked.

Gramp snorted, his white beard quivering. 'By Henry! I guess I know where we're located,' he said, his shrill voice echoing up and down Buffalo Creek. 'Wes and me and the others were out here last fall. We picked our spots right along this creek. Up close to where the water starts running. What's wrong up there? You'd think it was poison, the way you're acting.'

Jim looked at his partner, Steve Shane, a tall, blocky young man. 'We didn't mean to give you the wrong impression, Gramp,' Jim said. 'We've never been there. But we've heard that country up there is controlled by a big rancher.'

'It's controlled by them that owns it,' Gramp said sharply. 'And by Henry, we own a good piece of it along the creek. Or we will own it when we get proved up on it.'

'Do you think there'll be trouble?' Betty asked, looking from Steve to Jim.

'We hope not.'

Jim found himself wondering if the girl were comparing Steve and him, and he didn't like the thought. He knew what her conclusion would be. Steve was twenty-four, perhaps a couple of years older than Betty, well over six feet, fairly heavy-set, a big man with wavy brown hair and flashing blue eyes. On the other hand, Jim was an even six feet with straight brown hair and dark gray eyes. And Jim knew she wouldn't miss the deep weathering of his skin and the lines at the corner of his eyes where the sun had tried to add years to his thirty summers. If he took off his hat she'd see the white crease in the hairline above his forehead where a bullet had plowed the hair away and it had never come back.

He had seldom regretted the years that had piled up on him, but now, looking at Betty Ward and seeing the spark in Steve's eyes, he longed for a few of those years back.

Suddenly up on the bluff, which was little more than a steep slope here above the homesteader camp, a dozen riders appeared. Jim saw them against the bright moonlit sky only a second before the thunder of guns rolled up and down the creek.

Betty gave a short scream, while Wes Ward seemed suddenly turned to stone. Gramp broke into a run for his wagon, yelling a shrill curse at the riders on the bluff. Jim headed for his horse and found Steve at his side.

'What do you make of this?' Steve yelled.

'Nothing good,' Jim said.

They reached their horses and paused. Jim saw Gramp dive into his wagon and come out with a rifle which he put into immediate use. Ward and Betty had run to their wagon, but Jim didn't see Ward come out again. Jim had his gun in his hand but he only held it. The riders were well out of six-gun range and this was none of his affair, anyway. He and Steve had struck camp a half-mile downstream from the homesteaders.

The raiders rode back and forth along the top of the slope, firing noisily and apparently aimlessly. Jim frowned as he watched.

'They're using six-guns. Must not aim to hurt anybody.'

Steve nodded. 'I noticed. But Gramp has different ideas if he can shoot as straight as he's thinking.'

Other rifles began to speak from wagons around the camp. But the riders above continued their noisy firing, neither trying to come closer nor switching from their six-guns to rifles.

'Just trying to put a scare in the nesters,' Jim said. 'I can't say as I relish the idea.'

'Me, either.'

Jim glanced at his partner and wondered if he were thinking about Betty Ward, too.

'Let's bust it up.' Jim swung into the saddle.

Steve was already mounting. 'We may be biting off a pretty big chunk. But it won't be the first time.'

With a yell, they put their horses to a run and broke out of the camp and straight up the steep slope. The raiders were strung out for fifty yards along the top of the bluff, and they pulled up short when the two partners came charging at them. Then a shrill voice echoed along the slope.

'Scatter.'

The raiders broke in three directions and

4

were well out of .45 range when Jim and Steve reached the top of the bluff.

'Cowards!' Steve yelled, the glint of battle bright in his eyes.

'Take them,' Jim yelled, motioning upstream. 'I'll tackle these down here.'

Jim reined to his left, following three riders who had cut down the creek bank to the east. Others had headed south into the open prairie. He pushed his horse hard, determined to get close enough to identify the riders or read the brand on their horses. He admitted to himself that much of the fire that was driving him had been kindled by Betty Ward.

The three riders ahead swung down off the bluff, and Jim followed them to the bottomland along the creek bank. Here the ground was marshy in spots, and Jim held his horse close to the bluffs where footing was surer. He saw that he had gained considerable ground on the riders and apparently it was worrying them. They were twisting in their saddles to watch him.

Already Jim had discovered that one of the riders was much smaller than the others yet he apparently was the leader. And his strategy in dropping off the bluff suddenly became clear when he motioned one of the riders into a draw that cut into the chalk rock bluff.

Jim didn't slow his pace but he gripped his gun tighter. This could be an ambush. As he came even with the draw, he leaned low over

5

his saddle and tried vainly to pierce the shadows that cloaked the little ravine. But this wasn't the man he wanted to talk to. That little fellow who was handing out the orders was the one he had his mind set on cornering. And judging from the way he was overtaking the fleeing pair ahead, he stood a good chance of catching him.

He raced past the draw without hearing a shot or feeling the searing rip of a bullet. Jim guessed that the rider had been used merely as a decoy to pull him off the trail of the two up ahead.

Jim gained on the riders, and the big man turned and fired a shot at his pursuer. The bullet snapped past Jim's head, high and wide, just as the two ahead wheeled around a bend in the bluff.

Jim urged his horse to greater effort, but when he reached the turn, he caught a glimpse of only one horse going around another bend fifty yards farther down the creek bank.

He pulled up hard. When the two riders had made the first turn, they had been riding abreast. But Jim had seen only the big rider go around that second bend. Maybe the little fellow had forged ahead of his companion. And maybe he had turned off into some side pocket in the bluff, hoping Jim would trail his big companion.

Jim scanned the bluff to his right. There was a draw twenty yards ahead. He would lose out entirely if he were wrong, but he was going to have a look in that pocket.

Gripping his gun, he pushed his horse forward almost to the mouth of the draw. There he stopped and listened. There wasn't a sound. Maybe the little fellow had given him the slip. Or he might be waiting silently in ambush.

Jim knew he had lost too much time now to catch him if he had gone on, so he elected to play out his hunch. Slipping from the saddle, he ground-reined his horse and moved into the little gully on foot, keeping in the shadow as much as possible.

There was no place in the little draw for a man to hide except in some notch eroded out of the chalk rock walls. So far as Jim could remember there wasn't a tree along this creek for twenty miles. The moon hadn't reached its zenith yet and there was shadow along the eastern side of the gully. Jim guessed he'd find his man there if he were in this draw.

He zigzagged across the mouth of the gully to the shadows, making as uncertain a target as possible for any man waiting with a gun. But no shot came from the gully, and Jim began to doubt that the little fellow was here. One look at the far end of the draw dispelled any thought that he might have gone on through the ravine. That end was too steep for a rider to get out, at least without making a terrific racket. And Jim had heard no sound since pulling up here at the gully mouth.

He was about to walk out of the shadow and go back to his horse when he heard the shuffle of a horse's feet ahead. His nerves snapped tight. He hadn't guessed wrong. But where was the rider now?

'Drop your gun, mister.'

Jim had no choice, especially when he felt the muzzle of a gun nudge his back. He wondered fleetingly how the man could have slipped up behind him so quietly.

'Now turn around.'

Jim obeyed and got his first shock. The little fellow was only a youngster. He wasn't much over five feet even in his high-heeled boots. He wore faded Levis and a jacket that was much too big for him. A slouch-brim hat drooped over his face and shaded it from the moonlight that was beginning to climb above the gully wall.

'You're a little small to be filling man-sized boots, don't you think, kid?' Jim said easily.

'I'm bigger than you are while I've got this gun.'

Jim frowned. Even the kid's high-pitched voice betrayed his immaturity.

'What was the idea of that raid?' Jim asked, wondering what the kid planned to do with him.

'That's our business. And you might tell me what you're doing tailing us. You're no nester.'

'My partner and I happened to be visiting

8

the homesteader camp.'

'That didn't give you any call to come after us.'

'Maybe I'm sort of peculiar, kid. I don't like to have bullets flying around my ears even if they're not aimed to tag me. What did you expect to gain by scaring the wits out of those settlers?'

'Maybe pound a little sense into their heads. They're planning to settle above Bluestem, and there's no room up there for nesters.'

Jim watched the kid as the gun wavered slightly. 'I never heard of Bluestem.'

The kid relaxed more. 'It's just a new town. Only a month old, but it's booming.'

Jim was watching the hand holding that gun. Those fingers were longer and slimmer than a youngster's ought to be. Suddenly he forgot about the new town. His eyes shot up to the kid's face, the part that was showing under the slouch brim of the hat, and then down to the Levis stuffed into small boots. This was no kid. Even the floppy hat and the big jacket couldn't hide the telltale signs. This was a girl.

Anger rose in him, following the amazement that had disrupted his thinking. Here he stood, helpless at the hands of a girl.

'You can ride back now and tell those nesters to stay below Bluestem if they value their health,' the girl said.

The girl was waiting, apparently not thinking of using the gun to urge him on. Jim struck swiftly, a stab of his hand that caught the girl's wrist and twisted sharply. She cried out as the gun dropped into the grass.

'Now then,' he said, 'we're on even terms.'

'Even!' the girl snapped. 'You big ox! What's even about it?'

Jim grinned. 'Neither of us has a gun now.'

He still held her wrist, and with his free hand he reached up and jerked off her hat. Long black hair fell down over her shoulders. Moonlight fell on her face and he was startled at what he saw. Here was the second pretty girl he had encountered tonight. This one fell short of the beauty of Betty Ward, but she'd do. Her face was small and her nose turned up impudently. Jim couldn't be sure in the pale light, but he thought he saw a row of freckles over the bridge of that nose. Black eyes, bright with anger at the moment, bored into him.

'Why did you do that?'

Jim laughed. 'You didn't really think you could fool anyone, did you? There's too much girl about you.'

She jerked her arm. 'Let go of me!'

Jim held his grip. 'You know, you deserve a right good spanking for scaring those homesteaders like you did. Will you get it when you get home?'

'Nobody will dare lay a finger on me.'

With his free hand, Jim rubbed his chin. 'Well, now, maybe I'm not anybody, but I've got a finger on you. If you're not going to get a

10

walloping when you get home, maybe you ought to be taught a lesson right now.'

She gasped as he jerked her to him, smothering the gasp with his lips. She struggled fiercely, hammering him with her free hand. He held her tighter, barely feeling the blows. Then she stopped pounding him and her hand lay passively on his arm.

Reluctantly he released her and stepped back. Tears were in her eyes as she stared at him. Quickly, before he could dodge, she slapped him across the cheek, a jolt that rocked his head. But he only grinned.

She started to speak, choked on the words, and whirled toward her horse which was still hidden in the shadow of the chalk rock bluff.

Jim noticed that she wheeled upstream to the west. It upheld his conclusion that the raiders were from some ranch to the west, probably claiming the ground Gramp and the Wards had filed on.

He went back to his horse and headed for the homesteader camp.

Approaching the wagons, Jim saw that Steve had returned. He swung down and moved up close to the fire. 'I had a wild goose chase,' Steve said. 'How did you make out?'

Jim considered a moment and decided against telling these homesteaders it had been a girl he had overtaken. 'I caught up with one rider,' he said. 'Wouldn't say much, though. Something about there not being room above

11

Bluestem for nesters.'

'Bluestem!' Gramp snorted. 'That's the name of that new town we heard about. Supposed to be owned lock, stock, and barrel by a big ranch hog named Verdune. He considers homesteaders invaders.'

Jim shot a glance at his partner. Steve was looking steadily into the fire. Jim was remembering that tomorrow they would ride into the Flying V Bar and report to Claude Verdune for work.

CHAPTER TWO

The sharp trill of a meadowlark welcomed the first light of a new day and drove the sleep from Jim Taylor's eyes. Jim sat up in his blankets. The air was cool, almost cold, and there was a dampness along the creek that smelled like the refreshing breath of a thirsty land after a spring rain.

'Breakfast is waiting,' Steve yelled, pulling on his boots. 'And we're a mile from it.'

'She might keep it warm for you,' Jim said, grinning, and headed for the hobbled horses.

Only the growing light and the red streamers climbing into the sky foretold the coming of the sun when Jim and Steve headed up the creek. A flock of ducks rose suddenly from a little pool, the harsh quacks of the mallards contrasting sharply with the shriller cry of the teals.

Jim watched them wing away and tuned his ear to the other morning sounds. To the south, at the foot of the bluff, a proud prairie chicken voiced his morning crow. The meadowlarks up and down the creek filled the air with their music and the blackbirds chimed in with their throaty song.

He liked these birds and the sweet smell of the air. There was richness in this soil; the bluestem grass just starting to grow green along the creek proved it. He wondered if maybe at last he had found the place to send down his roots. He killed the thought abruptly. A man whose gun was for hire didn't take roots anywhere.

The homesteader camp was stirring when Jim and Steve rode up. Before they had reached the first wagon, Gramp came toward them at a trot. Jim reined up, seeing the calm routine of morning chores going on and wondering at Gramp's hurry.

'Go around to the south side of camp,' Gramp called, motioning excitedly. 'You mustn't come in from the east.'

Steve frowned. 'What difference does it make which side of camp we're on?'

Gramp came up to the horses, puffing from his run. 'It's bad luck to have the first company of the morning come in from the east,' he said solemnly.

At first Jim thought it was a joke. Then,

seeing the seriousness of Gramp's face, he realized that the old man was superstitions, that it was really important to him that his first company come into camp from some other direction.

'Sure, Gramp,' he said. 'We just weren't thinking.'

Steve leaned over his saddle horn. 'I still ain't thinking, I guess. What's the idea?'

Surprise flashed across Gramp's face. 'Don't tell me you've never heard that rule: First guest from the east in the morning; that's a sign you'd better take warning. I figure we're in for enough bad luck without wishing any more on us.'

Steve looked at Jim and frowned. Jim nodded. 'You're right, Gramp. A person can't afford to take chances. Come on, Steve, around to the south side of camp.'

Betty was at one of the four fires the homesteaders had going. Her face was rosy from her work over the chip fire and just as pretty as Jim had remembered. Her hair was done up in a bun on the back of her head, and it was even more lustrous in the sunlight than he had anticipated.

Jim dismounted quickly, but still he was behind Steve getting to the fire. From the look on Steve's face when he greeted Betty, Jim wondered if he would be wanting to move on to the Flying V Bar.

But when breakfast was over, Steve was the

14

one who was in a hurry to be riding. Gramp's invitation to stay with the wagon train while it moved up the creek to the new town of Bluestem fell on deaf ears.

It was Jim whose enthusiasm was waning. Somehow much of the glamour of the Flying V Bar job that had lured him through the last couple of months was gone this morning.

'We'll see you again, won't we?' Betty asked when they had mounted.

'You can bet your pretty head on that,' Steve said.

'Are you going to stay in this country?' Gramp asked.

'We expect to,' Jim said shortly.

'Going to homestead?'

Jim shook his head, wishing Gramp would stop his questions. 'We've got a job.'

'Ought to homestead,' Gramp said. 'The man who works for himself is a lot better off than the one who does the other fellow's chores. He won't have nothing to show for his work when he gets done.'

Jim nodded, recognizing the logic in Gramp's words. But Gramp couldn't know the job they had waiting or the wages it would bring. And, looking at Betty, he was thankful none of these homesteaders knew. Waving a hand, he reined his horse up the slope with Steve beside him.

It was a silent ride for several miles. Jim wondered if he and Steve were still thinking in

15

the same channels. He glanced at Steve, riding silently beside him, remembering how close they had been ever since they had met down in Texas.

Jim, the son of a storekeeper, had been attracted to the wild youngster the day he had ridden into town to hire his gun to the highest bidder in the range war that was boiling up. Possession of the water holes had been the core of the trouble, and before the thing had stopped, everyone in the area had been swept into it. Even Jim and his father had been dragged in because one faction thought the store was favoring the other in the goods it sold.

Even then Jim might have stayed out. But Steve came to town one night to spend an evening with Jim. When the opposition heard of it, they used it as an excuse to sweep down on the store and burn it, killing Jim's father.

Jim and Steve had fought side by side that night and they had been fighting together ever since. They had won that fight in Texas and it had given Steve a sense of superiority with his guns. With Steve's confidence, backed by his own and Jim's ability with guns, the partners had fought their way out of every tight spot except one. And in that one, guns had been no help.

Jim shook his head as he remembered. That defeat had marked the change in Steve, a change that had grown until Jim felt he scarcely

16

knew his old partner. It had come about this last winter sixty miles to the east along the Kansas border. The partners had saved up a stake and, at Jim's suggestion, they had decided to lay aside their guns and settle down.

Storekeeping was the only business Jim knew, and Steve had agreed to go in with him in a store in the little town of Sand Creek. But Sand Creek had ideas of its own about another store. The powers that controlled the destinies of the town didn't fight in the open with guns. But the result was the same. Jim and Steve were licked within six months.

It was then that Claude Verdune had come into the store. He had given himself a big build-up, leaving the impression that he was a little tin god out in the southwest corner of Nebraska. He had let it be known that he would need more hands when spring came, and Jim and Steve had jumped at the chance. Guns hadn't been mentioned but the partners had read the signs. Now the signs were becoming plain enough for a blind man to read.

'Do you think you'll like riding for Verdune?' Jim asked when they slowed their horses to a jog.

'I don't figure that's important,' Steve said. 'If he's half as big as he says he is, he'll be too tough for these nesters to handle.'

'You're sticking with the winners, is that it?' Jim asked, realizing that he had struck the core of the change in Steve.

17

Steve's jaw was set when he looked at Jim. 'We got tramped on in Sand Creek. I don't aim for it to happen again.'

'Did you ever stop to think who would get tramped on here?'

'I'm making sure it ain't me. The man with the guns is the man who will stay on top, and I figure Verdune will have the guns.'

'Guns make a lot of graves, Steve,' Jim said thoughtfully.

'I know it and I don't aim for one of them to be mine.' Steve's face softened a trifle. 'Maybe I sound hard-hearted, Jim. But I learned something in Sand Creek. If you don't look after Number One, nobody else is going to do it for you. I figure if a man is going to stay on top, he's got to pick the winning side and stick to it, right or wrong.'

'Maybe so,' Jim said, and touched his horse into an easy lope.

The size of the creek was dwindling noticeably as they rode to the west and north. It was a small stream fed by a thousand tiny oozing springs along its banks. The bluffs had drawn back a half-mile on either side of the creek and had given way to rolling hills. Meadows covered the flats back to these hills, meadows just beginning to turn green.

Jim could see why a rancher would want to hold this land. And he could see why homesteaders would flock in to plow it up. It was fertile land. To the north and east, beyond

18

the rim of hills hemming in the creek, the prairie stretched out, dry and flat and endless. And to the south and west it was hilly and filled with sagebrush and equally endless. To the north would be farmers and their families. And all the guns Verdune could command wouldn't keep them out. Jim had seen the last gasps of that struggle at Sand Creek. Here it was just the beginning, but the pattern was the same.

To the south the sand hills offered a different situation. Jim looked at them again. On the first slopes above the meadow land, he could see the twisted clumps of sagebrush. The man with the plow would hesitate before he tried to grub out those tree-like roots and plant his fields. Verdune might hold the sand hills.

Ahead, close to the creek, Jim saw a cluster of buildings and realized he was getting his first glimpse of Bluestem. Curiosity tugged at him. What kind of town had Verdune built? Jim had noticed several homesteads in the last few miles. Verdune might not be trying to shove the nesters off this land. Yet that girl last night had said there was no room for nesters above Bluestem. Apparently the town marked the dividing line between ranchers and homesteaders.

As they came nearer, Jim found it hard to believe the town was only a month or two old. At least a dozen frame buildings were along the one street, a street not yet beaten to a powdered dust. More buildings were in the process of going up at either end of the street. Back of these were a dozen soddies. A booming town, all right.

Jim and Steve went around the town, promising to come back later and look it over at their leisure. It was prairie above the town, unbroken as far as the eye could see, hills to the south, level land to the north.

They passed a small bunch of cattle with the Flying V Bar burned into their hips. They were fat and sleek and Jim understood a little more how Verdune must feel. This was a cattleman's paradise now. It would be his graveyard if the homesteaders got to it with their plows.

They found a tiny dugout close to the creek, but there was no sign of broken sod, even a garden patch, to indicate that the dugout belonged to a homesteader.

A mile above the dugout they hit a well worn trail that carried them up on the rim of hills to the south of the creek. There it straightened out, following the course of the creek but keeping off the bottom lands.

Following this trail, they came to the Flying V Bar. Jim would have known it from the description Claude Verdune had proudly given them when he was in Sand Creek. The house was a tall two-story building painted white. There was a small barn built of wood with a long sod shed behind it. Next to the barn was a small corral made of rock. Verdune had bragged about that stone corral, a corral that no animal could break through. From the looks of the rock, Jim guessed it had come from the nearby bluffs. Barbed wire fenced in the other corrals behind the barn. The long sod bunkhouse made an ugly contrast to the big house.

A tall, stoop-shouldered man came out on the porch of the house as they rode up, and Jim's eyes fell on the rifle slung in the crook of his arm. The man appraised them critically through sun-squinted eyes.

'What's on your mind?' he demanded gruffly.

'We're looking for Verdune,' Jim said.

'We've got a job here,' Steve added.

The man spat a stream of tobacco juice over the railing of the porch. 'Some more of those,' he said disgustedly. 'Come on in. But keep your nose clean.'

'Friendly cuss,' Steve murmured as they dismounted.

The man stepped back, watching Steve and Jim as they went into the house, then turned and crossed the yard toward the bunkhouse. The inside of the house was clean and neat but with only a minimum of furniture. A heavy-set man an inch or two shorter than Jim was standing at a side door of the room, and he came forward eagerly.

'Glad to see you boys,' he said, reaching out a soft short-fingered hand. 'How did the store venture end?'

'The store went broke flatter than a pancake,' Steve said. 'We're lucky to have a job to turn to.'

'You've got a good one here,' Verdune said heartily, a smile creasing his round face. He led them across the room and through the partition door. 'Have a chair, boys, and I'll tell you a little about your work.'

Jim seated himself and looked over the little office. It was clean but lacked the neat appearance of the outer room. Papers were scattered on a desk in the corner and some of them had slipped to the floor. A mounted prairie wolf's head snarled at the visitors from the wall over the desk.

'We bumped into some nesters heading this way,' Jim volunteered, watching Verdune's face as the rancher settled himself in a chair behind the desk.

Verdune leaned forward, his black eyes brightening as he ran a pudgy hand through his thinning brown hair. 'I've heard there were some coming to this part of the county,' he said, his voice softer than before. 'It looks like you boys may have some work to do.'

'We were in one range war,' Jim said quickly. 'We're not buying chips in another.'

Verdune fished a cigar out of a box on the desk and lighted it. 'I know you were in a scrap down in Texas. I find out about people before I give them jobs. But there will be no range war here. We have an organized county now with

22

law and order. The county seat, however, is more than thirty miles away. I can't run down there for the sheriff every time a nester infringes on my rights.'

'If there's not going to be any fighting, what kind of a job do you have for us?' Steve asked uneasily.

Verdune blew out a cloud of smoke. 'You're my insurance. I've got big plans, and those plans call for men of special abilities. I've been all over Nebraska, Kansas, and Colorado picking out the men I need. Each one has a special job.'

'Big plans usually call for a big place,' Jim said. 'The homesteaders are coming in fast. They'll squeeze you in.'

Verdune laughed. 'My boy, you completely underestimate me. I've planned on the homesteaders. The law won't allow me to hold my land by the gun, so I've got another way. A strictly law-abiding way. The nesters won't stay because they'll be too far from any town.'

'How about Bluestem?'

'Bluestem is my town,' Verdune said triumphantly. 'Every man in there is a man I've picked. This country is blanketed with my men. Outsiders won't find Verdune County a very friendly place.'

'I see they named the county after you,' Steve said, admiration in his voice.

'That's right,' Verdune said, puffing out another cloud of smoke. 'They did that because

23

I am one of the most prominent citizens in the county and because I was a representative to the state legislature from an eastern district before moving out here. A legislator is somebody. But I was only starting then. I'll be a much bigger man when I get things going my way here.'

Jim watched the pride swell in the big rancher. He had been aware of the importance in which Verdune held himself when he had been in Sand Creek, but here, where he was cock of the walk, it was an overbearing thing, stifling anyone coming in contact with it.

'With all these men you control,' he said finally, 'you're liable to find some who won't stay in line.'

Verdune laughed easily. 'There'll be some who'll get big ideas. But I've got an answer to that, too. You boys are it. Before I'm done, I'll own this entire corner of the county, maybe the whole west half. I'll be the richest man in the state.'

There was greed in the man now, greed that rose up and overshadowed the pride. Here, Jim realized, was the driving force that governed this big man. He had political experience, a fact that he could use as a guide to keep him from going too far outside the law. Jim knew he would be a hard man to curb.

He wondered what chance a homesteader like Ward or Gramp, struggling to make a living while he fought to fulfill a dream of being a

24

land owner, would have against a man like Verdune.

'If you wanted to be big, maybe you should have stayed in the legislature,' Jim said slowly.

'I could have; the voters liked me. But the legislature was paying only three dollars a day then, and I had nothing else to fall back on. There was more money in ranching out here, much more. At least there was until the sodbusters started coming.'

'What do we do right now?' Steve asked impatiently.

'Take your stuff down to the bunkhouse. You'll probably find my foreman, Bruce Noble, there. He'll put you at something. But I don't want you going very far away unless I say so.'

Jim and Steve started to rise but Verdune checked them. 'By the way, what do you know about these homesteaders you mentioned?'

'They said they had filed last fall on land along the creek up where the water starts running,' Jim answered. 'Last night we ran off a bunch of hoodlums who tried to scare the daylights out of them.'

The rancher frowned. 'Who was giving them the scare?'

'From what I heard, I thought maybe you could tell me.'

Verdune nodded. 'Maybe. If they take the hint and find some other place to squat, they'll spare themselves a lot of grief. But nesters usually take a lot of convincing.' He came around the desk. 'Bruce will fix you up down at the bunkhouse.'

That closed the subject. Dismissed, Jim and Steve went back through the big room and across the porch. Down in front of the bunkhouse, a man was leaning against the wall talking to the surly rifleman who had met them when they first came up.

As he crossed the yard, Jim sized up the new man. He was a squat, thick man with a square face. There was a dormant animosity in his pale blue eyes as he studied their approach. The man with the rifle moved on into the bunkhouse.

'Are you Noble?' Jim asked, stopping in front of the blocky man.

'Yeah.' The man showed stained, uneven teeth in a contemptuous grin. 'What do you want besides a bed and an easy job?'

'Verdune said you'd find something for us to do,' Steve put in quickly.

'The name is Mr. Verdune to you, bucko,' Noble said deliberately.

Color raced into Steve's cheeks and Jim watched for the explosion. But none came. Steve only nodded meekly.

Noble turned to Jim, a sneer on his broad face. 'How about you? Do you understand that, too?'

'When I think Verdune deserves a "Mr." before his name, I'll put it there,' Jim said evenly.

Dark anger flooded Noble's face. He moved a step toward Jim, fists balled, then stopped as the door of the house banged open and a girl came running across the yard to the bunkhouse, two long braids bouncing on her back.

At the corner of the bunkhouse she stopped, smiling mischievously.

'Aren't you going to introduce me, Bruce?'

At the sound of her voice the last doubt left Jim. This was the girl he had overtaken last night along the creek below the homesteader camp. The sunlight was even kinder to her than the moonlight had been. And there was a row of freckles over that pert little nose as he had suspected. But right now he didn't like the twinkle in her dark eyes as she watched him and waited for Noble to make the introductions.

'I don't know their names, Stormy,' Noble said uncomfortably. 'I reckon they're a couple more the boss has hired.'

The girl laughed, her braids dancing across her back as she turned her head. 'Maybe I should do the introducing then. Dad told me who they are. And he wants to see you at the house, Bruce.'

Jim tried to keep abreast of things. This girl—Stormy, Noble had called her—was evidently Claude Verdune's daughter.

'So you know us, do you?' Steve said, grinning as he warmed to the task of

27

acquainting himself with another pretty girl.

'Dad told me who you were,' she said to Steve. Then she turned to Jim and her eyes flashed. 'He didn't need to tell me who Jim Taylor is.'

'Do you know him?' Steve demanded in amazement.

'Seems like we've met. Haven't we, Jim?'

Jim knew his neck and face were beginning to redden. Stormy Verdune was not one to take a defeat without retaliation. And apparently she considered that incident last night a defeat, at least to her pride. He glanced at his partner. Steve was looking at him as though he were seeing a ghost.

'Jim?' Steve repeated, looking back at the girl. 'Aren't you getting pretty familiar with him?'

She smiled knowingly at Jim. 'Not half as familiar as he gets with me.'

'Holy smoke!' Steve exploded. 'What's she talking about, Jim?'

Jim knew he had to speak up in his own defense.

'She was the kid I overtook last night after the raid. She got the drop on me and I took the gun away from her.'

Noble spun away from the porch where he had been talking to Verdune. Stormy saw him and turned back to Steve. She started to speak, then looked at Jim and winked.

'Let's let him guess what happened, Jim,' she

28

said, and wheeled toward the house, running as she had come.

'Holy smoke, Jim!' Steve ejaculated, staring at his partner.

'You said that before,' Jim reminded him.

'If I hadn't known you for five years, Jim—'

'I outwitted her last night and she had to get even,' Jim explained. 'Let's let it go at that.'

'I reckon we'd better,' Steve said dubiously. 'Sleeping dogs usually bite when they're kicked.'

Noble reached the bunkhouse and stopped squarely in front of Jim. 'The boss has a job for you, Taylor,' he said.

'Sounds good to me,' Jim said, hoping it would take him away from the Flying V Bar.

'You're to go to town or wherever those nesters are now and stick with them to see what they do,' Noble said. 'You'll report back here Sunday morning unless they head upstream before then. You're to come here and tell us if they do.'

It sounded good to Jim. Yet he knew Verdune could keep a check on the homesteaders without assigning a man to watch them.

'What about Steve?' he asked.

'He stays here. I've got another job for him. You won't need any help.'

Jim turned toward his horse in front of the house. He saw Steve's envious eyes on him and knew he was thinking of Betty Ward.

29

Jim found Ward's wagons just to the east of the town. The teams were unhitched and it looked as if there was to be an overnight camp at that site.

Jim wondered about that. There was plenty of time to reach their land before the sun went down. And if they were like most homesteaders, they could hardly wait until they got to their new homes.

He reached the wagons and dismounted. Betty Ward met him, and her eyes showed surprise and a welcome that brought back that giddy feeling.

'I didn't expect to see you again so soon,' she said.

'You never know what to expect from me. Why aren't you moving on to your homesteads?'

She sighed, and there was exasperation in her voice. 'It's Gramp. This is Friday, you know. And he isn't going to start anything on Friday that he can't finish before the day is over.'

'That's right, by Henry!' Gramp put in as he came around the nearest wagon. 'It's bad luck to start something on Friday that you can't finish before the sun goes down. And I ain't expecting to finish homesteading my hundred and sixty that soon.'

'That's just a silly superstition, Gramp,'

Betty said impatiently.

'That's what you call it. I know it's a fact. Why I knowed a fellow back in sixty-one that got married on Friday. He was killed at Shiloh.'

Vexation burned in the girl's cheeks. 'I suppose you think getting married on Friday caused him to get killed.'

'By Henry, it didn't keep him alive,' Gramp said in a tone that plainly declared he considered his point made.

But for the seriousness of Gramp's face, Jim would have laughed. In a way, though, he was glad for the delay in the homesteaders' plans. It was only postponing trouble. But during that postponement, a solution might appear.

'When are you moving on?' he asked.

'Sunup in the morning,' Gramp said quickly. 'We'll get settled on our own land in time to go to meeting Sunday morning and praise the Lord for being good to us.'

'Dad says we ought to find Mr. Adley, the locator,' Betty said, 'and have him show us exactly where our land is.'

'I know where mine is, by Henry!' Gramp said vehemently. 'That slick-tongued Press Adley might try to push me off on some sand pile, but I know the quarter I picked out.'

'The locator ought to be able to show you your exact boundaries,' Jim put in. 'It might be a little awkward if you built your house on somebody else's land.'

Gramp gave ground reluctantly. 'Well,

31

maybe you're right. But I wouldn't trust him as far as I could throw a bull by the tail.'

'I think I'll ride into town and look it over,' Jim said. 'Maybe I can find this fellow Adley.'

'He's not in his office,' Betty said. 'Dad went there to see him. Dad thinks he's trying to avoid us.'

Gramp snorted. 'Wes is always looking for the black side of things. And he'll find the black side of humanity when he finds Press Adley.'

Jim grinned and picked up the reins of his horse. He wasn't particularly interested in finding Adley but he did want to look over Claude Verdune's town.

When Jim dismounted in front of the general store, he had already discovered that there were more buildings in the process of going up than there were already completed.

The general store where he had stopped was one of the finished buildings and, according to the sign, was operated by Tom Biggs. Just south of the store was a big building that Jim guessed to be either a meeting hall or a schoolhouse. A sign tacked on the door read 'Dance Saturday night.' A hardware and a blacksmith shop down the street were completed. A lumber yard and a drug store were well started, and just across the street was the Verdune House, nearly finished.

Seeing the hotel reminded Jim that he hadn't had any dinner, and he crossed the street. The dining room was open, doing a big business. Jim found an empty chair at the long table and sat down, looking out on the bustling street. A bare spot on a bare prairie that had suddenly become a booming town! It just didn't add up.

Jim had dinner, tossed down his quarter, and went back outside. From the veranda of the hotel he saw another small building part way down the block that he hadn't noticed before. He went that way, finding half a dozen men working there.

'Going to be a printing office,' one worker volunteered when Jim asked.

'Bluestem is going to have a paper. That fellow over there is the editor, Eddie Lowe.'

Jim followed the pointing finger to a thin, wiry man with sandy hair and blue eyes and cheeks sunken in as though he had been on a starvation diet. He was handling a saw as if he had never seen one before. Jim crossed leisurely to him.

'Looks like you'll be printing a paper before many days,' he said.

The man looked up, and Jim saw that he was young. His eyes glowed with excitement. 'Sure will. Want to buy a subscription?'

Jim grinned at his enthusiasm. 'I'll wait till I see the paper. Know where I can find a fellow named Adley?'

Lowe rubbed his chin that needed a shave. 'I'm new here. Don't know many people yet. Tom Biggs would be the man to ask.'

33

Jim thanked him and started to turn away.

'Be glad to put you down for a subscription to the Bluestem *Bugle*,' Lowe said eagerly.

'Later maybe.' Jim angled across the street toward Biggs' general store. He instinctively liked Eddie Lowe, although there was something about him that made Jim nervous.

He wasn't too concerned about finding Press Adley. But Betty Ward had wanted to get hold of the locator and he had agreed to look for him.

Biggs' store was spacious, evidently built with an eye to a future city. Tom Biggs himself was a tiny man, less than five and a half feet tall, bald, with piercing blue eyes. Biggs looked Jim over carefully before he said anything, and when he spoke, there was an antagonistic edge to his voice.

'You're with that bunch of nesters, ain't you?'

Irritation nagged at Jim. 'I don't happen to be. But even if I was, there's no law against homesteaders.'

'That's according,' Biggs said, rubbing a hand over his bald noggin. 'There is against that particular bunch.'

Jim's interest surged up. 'Why is Ward's outfit being singled out?'

Biggs turned a penetrating glare on Jim. 'Either you don't belong to that bunch or else you're just playing dumb. They're the first outfit to pick out land above here. That will

34

mean trouble and we don't want trouble in this country. We figure the easiest way to avoid it is to boycott anybody with ideas of settling upstream.'

'Just who do you mean by "we"?'

'The storekeepers in town. We have agreed not to sell to Ward's outfit. We aim to have a peaceful town here.'

Hot words surged to Jim's lips but he bit them back. He wanted to ask the impudent little merchant how much Claude Verdune was paying him to boycott Ward's wagon train. Verdune had made his brag that this was his town and every man in it was picked. Apparently it wasn't an empty boast.

'Is Press Adley in town?' Jim asked finally.

'He was over in the drug store the last I knew.'

Jim went out into the street where the grass was not yet completely worn away and angled across to the drug store next to the Verdune House. Workmen were fitting windows and plastering in the front part of the building. There was no business here, but behind a partition toward the back of the big room, men were talking above the rattle of hammers. Jim knew what he would find there. There was no saloon in town, but this back room of the drug store was a good substitute.

Three men were at a little table behind the partition playing cards, and Jim picked the flabby man in the brown suit as the one he was

35

looking for. Ignoring the other two, he spoke to the heavy-set man.

'Are you Adley?'

The man looked up lazily, taking a dead cigaret out of the corner of his mouth. 'Yeah. What's on your mind?'

'Some people want to see you. They say you located them last fall up the creek from here and they want to be sure about their boundaries.'

Understanding ran over Adley's flabby face and he looked back at his companions, throwing them a sly wink that Jim didn't miss. 'Sure. I always see to it my customers are located where they ought to be. Where are they?'

'Camped just east of town.'

'Tell them I'll be right out.' Adley looked back at his cards.

'I'm not telling them anything, Adley,' Jim said, irritation working up in him. 'You're going to do that. Let's go.'

Surprise washed over the locator's face. He looked up at Jim, then back at his companions who were grinning broadly. 'Now look who's talking. You're forgetting you're not back in some little eastern town. You don't talk to people here like that.'

'Maybe you don't. I do.'

Anger stirred red spots in Adley's cheeks. 'You don't either, bucko.'

Jim knew something was wrong. If Adley

36

had played square with the homesteaders, he wouldn't be so reluctant now to show them their land. The conviction broke a tide of anger washing over Jim.

'Are you coming, Adley, or do I have to take you?'

The big locator shoved back his chair and got to his feet. 'When anybody takes me anywhere, it will be somebody bigger than you.'

'I may change your mind if you don't come of your own accord.'

'I'll come when I get ready. No two-bit nester is going to tell me what to do.'

'I'll take you then,' Jim said, and grabbed a handful of Adley's shirt front.

With a curse, Adley swung wildly with both fists. Jim had expected it. He dodged and his fist shot back, landing with a jolt he felt all the way to his shoulder. He had to release his grip to keep from tearing the locator's shirt as Adley rocked back against the wall.

'Change your mind?' he asked as Adley leaned there, letting the surprise drain out of his face.

'I might as well go one time as another,' the locator muttered.

Jim nodded, amazed that the argument was over so quickly, and turned back through the partition door. Adley came after him, muttering under his breath, and they went into the street together.

Gramp saw them as they rode out of town

and had Wes Ward at the edge of camp to meet them. Excitement was buzzing through the wagons.

'Where was he hiding?' Gramp demanded. 'Under a wet rock?'

'Sopping up beer and playing cards,' Jim said. 'He wasn't exactly anxious to come. But he's ready now to show you your places.'

'I know where mine is,' Gramp retorted. 'All he can show me is my exact boundaries.'

'There are a lot of things I can show you,' Adley snapped.

Gramp sparred immediately. 'And I can show you a few things, too, I reckon.'

'Let's get down to business,' Ward said. 'We'll get our horses and be right with you.'

'Got the description of your land?' Adley asked.

Gramp patted his shirt pocket. 'Right here. But I don't need no paper. I remember it. Northeast quarter of twenty-two, township six. Buffalo Creek cuts right through the middle of my quarter.'

Adley grinned and there was satisfaction in his face. 'Are you sure you're on twenty-two?'

'By Henry, I guess I know the numbers of my land. What's eating you?'

'Twenty-two is not on the creek. It's two miles north.'

Unbelief swept over Gramp and Ward. Jim wasn't surprised at the announcement. He looked at the grin of pure enjoyment on

Adley's flabby face, and it ran through his mind that the locator was probably another of Verdune's picked men and this was a cut and dried scheme.

'You're a liar!' Gramp burst out. 'I saw the creek running through my land.'

'You weren't looking at your land,' Adley said easily. 'If you were, you didn't see a creek. The creek's two miles south of you on thirty-four.'

'I don't believe it,' Gramp yelled.

Adley, complete master of the situation now, calmly dug a map out of his pocket. 'Take a look,' he said, holding out the map. 'You can see the course of Buffalo Creek. It comes into Township Six on section nineteen, cuts across twenty-nine and twenty-eight, then down into thirty-three, thirty-four and thirty-five and on into section one of Township Seven. That proof enough?'

Gramp and Ward were staring at the map, and Jim could guess what was going through their minds. Their hopes of having choice land was gone. They were the victims of an old game that dishonest locators had played with eager land seekers wherever land was open to homesteaders. Many a locator had shown the same quarter to dozens of home seekers, collected his fee for locating them, then let them find to their sorrow that they had filed on some undesirable piece of parched prairie. Jim was surprised that Gramp hadn't demanded

39

more proof than Adley's word that the land he saw and the numbers he filed on were the same piece of land.

Ward, still looking at the map, nodded in despair, and Gramp, finally convinced, threw down the map and lunged toward Adley's horse.

'I'll skin you alive, you blubber-headed skunk!'

Adley reined his horse back. 'Keep away from me, you old goat!' he snapped. 'You've got your land. Take it and like it!'

There were tears in Gramp's eyes as he lunged toward the locator again, intent on dragging him off his horse. Adley had no stomach for such an encounter, even with a small man like Gramp who was thirty years his senior. As he jerked his horse back again, he whipped a gun from under his coat. Jim, a spectator up to this point, became a part of it now.

'Easy, Adley,' he said sharply, and his own gun was in his hand. 'If you want to use that gun, turn it my way.'

Gramp had stopped at sight of the gun, and Adley, for the second time in an hour, refused to accept Jim's challenge. 'I'm not a gunfighter,' he said lamely.

'Then don't play with guns,' Jim snapped. 'Now what's to prevent Ward and Gramp from letting their homesteads go and taking preemptions on the creek land?'

40

'The creek's already taken,' Adley said, and a trace of satisfaction came back on his face. 'They've got good land. Sandy loam.'

'I don't want sand,' Gramp said, and there was a sob in his voice.

Jim felt sorry for the old man. This was Gramp's last chance and he was being cheated out of it.

'You'd better get back to your card game, Adley,' Jim said. 'We don't want you stinking up the camp.'

With a sneering laugh, Adley wheeled his horse and loped back into town. Jim dismounted, leading his horse to the wagons. Betty met him there.

'I heard,' she said miserably. 'What are we going to do?'

'I can't say right now what would be best,' Jim said. 'You can tell better what to do after you look at the land your folks really filed on. Maybe you'd ought to give up here and try some other place.'

She shook her head. 'Gramp will never give up. Neither will the rest, unless it would be Dad. None of them have ever owned land. We've never had more than enough to live on. After about so much pushing around, you get all you can stand.'

'Is that how you folks feel?'

'Exactly. We've got a chance to own land and be somebody. Nobody can look down on us if we own land along the creek. Gramp says it's

41

the best.'

'You can be somebody without owning land along the creek.'

Betty looked straight at Jim, and he was startled at the determination he saw in her eyes and the tilt of her chin. 'Maybe you've never been down and out. When you get a chance to get what you want, you don't give up without a fight.'

'If the creek is already taken, you'll have to be satisfied with something else.'

She shook her head. 'Not satisfied. We may have to take it, but we'll never be satisfied till we get the best. We've had enough leftovers.'

Jim had seen the same pride in Gramp. If Gramp were younger or Betty were a man, there would be trouble along Buffalo Creek before Verdune got rid of Ward's homesteaders. Looking at the girl now and thinking of Gramp, he wasn't so sure there wouldn't be, anyway.

'I didn't think there were such scoundrels as Press Adley,' she said bitterly.

'You'll find his kind everywhere you go. You were just unlucky to have any dealings with him.'

'It's always his kind that gets to the top. I wish there was some way of beating him.'

Jim watched her as she stared out over the town. There was a thoughtful look, granite-hard with determination, on her face. It told Jim plainer than words that she really meant she wished there was a way to get higher than Adley; to beat him at his own game.

'Let's forget Adley,' he said finally. 'I saw a sign on the meeting hall door in town. There's a dance there tomorrow night. Why don't we go and show them up on the dance floor?'

The deep thoughtful look vanished as she smiled at him. 'Sounds like a wonderful idea, Jim. We'll get to meet people who won't look down on us. They can't all be like Press Adley.'

'We can be thankful for that,' Jim said.

He realized how much his sympathies were swinging to the homesteaders. This wasn't the way he had planned it when he and Steve had agreed to work for Verdune. He had been satisfied with himself then. But today he had seen the seeds of war sown, and he wondered where he would be when the harvest came.

CHAPTER FOUR

The wagons didn't roll at sunup as Gramp had predicted. But the homesteaders themselves were moving. Jim saw horses, never meant for anything more refined than harness, put under saddles as several of the men, headed by Gramp and Ward, prepared to ride out to have a look at their land. Jim saddled up and joined them.

'If I had that wobble-jawed skunk by the neck, I'd drag him all the way out there,'

43

Gramp raved as he climbed up on a raw-boned bay.

Jim looked over the group. Anyone could have tagged them as homesteaders. Only Wes Ward rode straight in the saddle with an ease that was entirely missing in the others. Cavalry, Jim thought, remembering Gramp's remark about the bayonet wound Ward had received in the war.

'I say to string him up if the land he shows us ain't nothing but sand and sagebrush,' one bearded man grumbled.

'What to?' another snapped. 'Ain't a tree within forty miles.'

'Trouble will get us nowhere,' Ward said. 'Let's make the best of it.'

'There ain't no best to it,' Gramp snorted. 'Mark my words, it will be a dry sand pile he'll try to push off on us.'

They reined up in front of the Verdune House and half of them dismounted. Gramp moved up on the veranda and Jim caught him there.

'I'll get Adley,' he said, and went inside.

Calling Adley out might create an explosive situation. And Gramp had a pretty short fuse this morning.

The desk clerk didn't respond until Jim had rung the bell twice. Then he showed up, yawning sleepily.

'What do you want?'

'What room is Press Adley in?'

44

The clerk rubbed the sleep out of his eyes. 'He doesn't get up this early.'

'That's too bad. What's his room number?'

The clerk frowned, then pointed down the hall. 'Number six.'

It took some lively pounding to bring Adley to the door. When he did appear, his flabby face was furrowed by a scowl.

'What do you want at this unholy hour?' he demanded.

'It's not the hour that's unholy,' Jim said softly. 'It's some people. There are a dozen men outside waiting for you to show them what kind of a double-cross you pulled on them.'

'Let them find their land themselves.' Adley started to push the door shut.

Jim slammed a shoulder against the door, shoving it in and sending Adley reeling toward the bed.

'You showed them wrong once, Adley. You're going to show them right this time. The mood they're in, you won't live to make very many more mistakes.'

Adley dropped on the edge of the bed. 'I haven't had breakfast. They'll have to wait.'

'Wrong again, Adley,' Jim said, patience running out of him. 'You'll do the waiting—for your breakfast. Get dressed and be quick about it.'

The locator flipped a glance at his gun in the shoulder holster hanging on the chair, then apparently thought better of it. He dressed

45

quickly and went out of the room ahead of Jim.

Adley was surly and short-tempered when he wheeled his horse out of the livery stable. Jim rode beside him as they headed out of town.

It was a half-hour ride to the land Adley said belonged to the homesteaders. All their land joined, forming a big block on the prairie. The dirt was a sandy loam as Adley had said, but there was no water in sight. Good land, though, Jim thought.

'How much rain do you get here?' Ward asked, looking over the land and nodding in satisfaction.

'Enough,' Adley said sulkily.

'What's your idea of enough?' Gramp demanded.

'More than you deserve,' the locator snapped, and started to rein his horse back toward town.

'You lop-eared baboon!' Gramp roared. 'You ain't the good Lord. He'll give us what we deserve without you deciding what it is. Will we get enough rain to raise corn and millet?'

'That's according to how thick you plant it,' Adley said sullenly. 'This ain't Iowa; I'll tell you that for sure. You won't get a downpour every week.'

'We'll take it,' Ward said with finality.

Gramp snorted. 'Ain't nothing else we can do, I reckon. But I'm taking it just so I can be close enough to fight for what is mine.'

'This quarter is all that's yours,' Adley said

sharply. 'You won't have to fight for that.'

'I picked out a quarter on the creek,' Gramp said flatly. 'That's mine and I'll get it.'

Adley looked over the group of men behind Gramp. Those men weren't looking at the land now. They were staring at the locator. Adley shifted uneasily in his saddle, then reined around toward town. Nobody stopped him.

Betty was the first to meet the riders when they got back to the wagons. Her question, aimed at Gramp and Ward, seemed to include Jim, too.

'Is it as bad as you thought?'

'Good land,' Ward said. 'Might be dry in the summer, though.'

'Are we going to move out there today?' she asked.

Ward looked up at the sun, then glanced at Gramp. Jim realized that the final decision would come from the old man.

Gramp shook his head. 'We ain't starting a new job on an old week. We'll stay here, go to meeting tomorrow, and move out to our land first thing Monday morning.'

There was no dissenting voice, even though Jim saw disappointment on some of the men's faces. He dismounted and led his horse over behind Gramp's wagon. Betty fell in beside him.

'What do you think, Jim?'

'About the same as your dad does. The soil is all right if you just get enough rain.'

47

'The creek land would be better.'

Jim nodded. 'Of course it would.'

'We'll get it then. We bargained for the best and we'll have it.'

Jim stripped the saddle off his horse. 'Better wait and see what the situation is along the creek.'

'I'm glad we're staying here tonight,' she said, her face brightening. 'We'll be close to town and the dance. I haven't been to a dance in ages. Seems like we've been traveling for months, every day just like the one before.'

'The dances out here start about dark,' Jim said.

'I won't be late,' she promised.

True to her word, she was ready and waiting when Jim came to Ward's wagon shortly after sundown. They walked the short distance to town in the gathering twilight. Lights were springing up here and there in the sod houses behind the row of false-fronted store buildings.

The meeting hall was open and the crowd was beginning to gather when Jim and Betty went inside. It wasn't the gay crowd Jim had expected. There was an air of tight restraint in the people who came through the door, found seats on the benches along the walls, and waited for the music to begin. From their dress, Jim tabbed most of those present as homesteaders.

Then the Flying V Bar riders arrived. They came arrogantly, noisily, led by their foreman,

Bruce Noble. They left no doubt that they considered themselves the kingpins. Most of the men were without partners. But Steve Shane had a partner. That fact didn't surprise Jim, but his partner did. Dressed like a lady with the pigtails done up in a bun on her head, Stormy Verdune had blossomed out from the impish rogue who had made him backpeddle yesterday morning. She was pretty enough, Jim thought, to make a man forget himself. But the flash in those black eyes was warning enough, at least to a man who had been burned once.

Two big lamps hanging from the ceiling were lighted and a dozen small bracket lamps along the wall reflected their beams from the polished mirrors behind them. A couple of fiddlers took their places next to the organ and tuned their instruments. Then the man on the organ stool pulled out all the stops and gave the pedals a couple of hard pushes.

'Looks like we're going to start on a loud fast one,' Jim said softly, his eyes still on his old partner and Stormy Verdune.

'Who's the girl with Steve Shane?' Betty asked, following the direction of Jim's gaze.

'That's Claude Verdune's girl.'

'She certainly dresses well,' Betty said.

For the first time Jim really noticed the dress Stormy was wearing. It was blue satin, soft and clinging, and it fairly shouted its expensiveness. He wondered if he were imagining the jealous note in Betty's voice. Betty's dress was neat and pretty enough to please Jim, but there was nothing expensive about it.

'Silks and satins for those with money to throw to the birds,' Jim said lightly.

'Some day it won't be that way,' Betty said tightly, and Jim saw again that far-away, thoughtful look in her eyes.

With a mighty wheeze from the organ and a scraping of fiddles, the music started on a schottische and Jim came to his feet.

'Shall we give it a try?'

She smiled, the determined look gone as quickly as it had fled yesterday afternoon. 'I didn't walk over here just to sit and listen.'

The music was good, better than Jim had expected, and he enjoyed himself. The schottische gave way to a waltz and the waltz to a quadrille. The caller for the quadrille was a thin hollow-cheeked man with a sonorous voice that droned over the room.

'All of the ladies to the right of the ring
When you get there, balance and swing
When you have swung, honor the call
It's allemande left and promenade all.'

Jim found himself in a square with Steve and Stormy. With twice as many men as women, the competition for partners was keen. Quadrilles gave the stag line a chance to cut in. The caller changed his chant, and as Steve came between Jim and Betty on his way around to swing Stormy, Bruce Noble stepped in ahead of him and Steve was out.

50

'Tough luck, Steve,' Jim said, grinning.

Steve laughed. 'Don't worry about me. "I'll get another one, a better one, too!"' he said, quoting a line the caller had used not long before.

On the next call when Jim came around to swing Betty, Steve had neatly cut him out. He made a friendly pass at Steve, then stepped back, content to watch for a while.

Another man cut Noble out, and as he was swinging Stormy, she caught Jim's eye over her partner's shoulder and winked. He waited until Stormy and her partner separated to come around to swing, then stepped in.

'Is four different partners for one dance too many?' he asked.

She laughed. 'The more the merrier. I thought you'd be around to speak before this.' There was a teasing note in her voice.

Halfway through the dance, Jim felt a hand on his shoulder and turned to look at Noble, whose face was drawn down in a heavy scowl. Noble spoke to Stormy.

'You've got to be more careful, Stormy,' he said in a voice intended to carry over the room. 'He's beginning to smell like a sodbuster.'

It was a challenge. Jim couldn't ignore it. The dancers close by turned expectant eyes on Jim and edged back.

'I suppose you think you smell better?' he said sharply.

'At least I didn't bring a nester girl here.'

51

The emphasis he put on the word 'nester' made it sound like an oath. Even if Jim had felt like avoiding a fight, he couldn't do it now. No man spoke in that tone about another man's girl and went unchallenged.

'No nester girl would stoop low enough to be seen with you,' Jim said.

Noble wheeled toward Jim, and the nearby dancers scattered like quail before a diving hawk. His fist shot out at Jim, but it only grazed his cheek. Jim's return punch struck home, rocking the Flying V Bar foreman back against the wall. Noble was a bigger man than Jim, but when he recoiled from the wall, Jim stood toe to toe with him, slugging it out and giving more than he was taking.

Noble tried desperately to hold his ground, but inch by inch he was forced back by Jim's stinging, accurate jabs. Back to the wall finally, he braced and made a last stand. But the advantage was all Jim's now. There had been no call for Noble's challenge so far as Jim could see, and there was no leniency in Jim now. His fists smashed through Noble's guard repeatedly and slashed his face. He wondered how much the big foreman was going to take before he gave in.

Then suddenly Jim was struck from behind with a force that drove him to his knees. He twisted to see a new man, who had been pointed out to him as Ross Harder, lunging at him, following up the sneak blow he had landed.

Rolling, Jim escaped Harder's charge and came to his feet. But he was outmanned now, for Noble, with a wild roar, charged in on him from one side while he was fending off Harder from the other.

Punishment rained on Jim. Still he managed to catch Harder with a blow that knocked him back against the wall. But he was unable to follow up his advantage because Noble bored in on him then.

Jim saw Harder's hand slide down his leg, obviously searching for a gun. But all guns had been checked at the door tonight. The move marked Harder, though, for what he was—a gunhand.

Faced by a furious twin attack, Jim was backed across the room till he hit the wall. He was absorbing brutal punishment, but his anger at Harder's sneak attack refused to let him admit defeat. The crowd for the most part was silent now, the homesteader majority sensing that Jim was fighting their fight against Noble, the symbol of Verdune's Flying V Bar.

The room began to grow hazy before Jim's eyes as his guard weakened and the blows kept pouring in. He felt himself slipping down the wall.

He was only half conscious when the fists finally stopped pounding and Betty helped him to his feet and guided him outside. The cool spring air cleared his brain rapidly and he took

53

stock of the beating he had received. There could be no doubt who had been the victors. Jim had the feeling that the first blow of the pending war had been struck.

CHAPTER FIVE

The Flying V Bar was a quiet place until the men rode in Sunday noon. Stormy Verdune had waited anxiously for the last two hours for their return from town. When they did come in, she met Claude Verdune on the porch.

'Did you see Jim Taylor?'

'That's what I went to town for,' Verdune said sullenly.

Stormy saw the signals. Something had gone wrong. It must be more than just a refusal by Jim Taylor to work on the Flying V Bar. Verdune hadn't been very enthusiastic about asking Jim to come back to the ranch. He had given in only to persistent arguments from Stormy. But now he was in a rage.

He stamped across the porch and through the big room to his office. Stormy followed. Angry or not, he could give her an account of the trip.

'Did Taylor put a burr under your saddle?' she asked.

'He'll regret the day he set foot in this country,' Verdune grated. 'The gall of him! He says he's going to start a store to sell to those

54

nesters aiming to settle on my grass.'

'A store?' Stormy said in surprise. 'Where is he going to put it?'

'He doesn't have any place to put it. But I've got a feeling he may find a place. Of course, I can get rid of it. But it might be nasty business.'

'You'll have to be careful how you do it,' Stormy warned seriously. 'People will be watching every move you make now. And they are the ones who vote.'

'Don't you think I know that?' Verdune shouted angrily. 'I was in politics before you were big enough to know a ballot box from a shoe box. But I can't let him operate a store right under my nose. The nesters would pour in here like water out of a bucket. And I don't intend to let this land get away from me.'

'Don't you want to go back in the legislature?'

'I've got to go back. Since the legislature passed that infernal herd law, I'm up against it. I can't keep the nesters out of my hair. When I get back in Lincoln I'll do something about that law.'

'You won't be elected if you antagonize the voters,' Stormy said solemnly. 'Nothing scares off a voter like a shady deal.'

Verdune nodded impatiently. 'Sure, sure, I know. You don't need to preach to me. But if I let the sodbusters tear up all my grass, those laws I want to get passed won't do me any good. I've made plans, Stormy, while you were

55

in school. I'm going to make this ranch the biggest thing in the state. And I'll be the richest man.'

Stormy walked to the door of the office and looked out, ignoring Verdune's muttering behind her. Her one hope of preventing a war and Verdune's one hope of saving the Flying V Bar was to get him back in the legislature. That hadn't been altogether her idea. It had originated with Chester Fyfe, the bright young lawyer she had met while at school back east.

She turned back to Verdune. 'Chester says you mustn't make any open move against the homesteaders now. And Chester is a master of politics.'

'When is this Chester-know-it-all going to get here?' Verdune demanded irritably. 'It's been Chester this and Chester that till I'm getting sick of it. Let him come here and give his advice first hand.'

'He'll be here the middle of May. You'll be a cinch to win the election with Chester managing your campaign. Chester says to let the homesteaders alone and you'll probably be able to buy them out after they have been on their land long enough to pay out on it. That will give you a legal title to the land.'

'You let me worry about how to handle the homesteaders,' Verdune said. 'It's harder to get land than it is to keep it once you've got it. And I've got this now. I won't need your precious Chester's help getting through the primary

56

election, either, since I don't have any opposition on my ticket.'

'You'll have opposition in the general election. Chester says it takes a lot of planning to win a campaign. He wants to get an early start.'

Stormy left the office, fighting a sense of futility. With Jim Taylor backing them, the homesteaders wouldn't give up as easily as it had seemed they surely would when faced with the obstacles Verdune had placed in their way.

The situation looked no brighter two days later when Noble came back from town with Press Adley in tow. He headed straight for Verdune's office and Stormy followed. Noble was bursting with news and Stormy could see that it wasn't good news.

Verdune looked up from his desk and grunted.

'Well, I got him,' Noble said, and dropped in a chair. 'Things are sure busting in town. Ward's outfit of nesters have moved up on their land north of the creek, and Taylor has started digging for the foundation of his store.'

Verdune dropped his cigar on the desk, unlit. 'Where?'

'On that lot you sold to Hackett. Seems that Hackett sold to Taylor and pulled out.'

Verdune twisted the cigar in his fingers. 'That's a fine mess,' he said finally. 'Adley, you located those nesters on that land. Is there any way to get them off?'

57

Adley, his face flushed from drinking, laughed hoarsely. 'That was your idea to show them the creek, then plant them up there. You said you didn't want them on the creek.'

'I don't want them where they are, either. Can't they be kicked off?'

'Sure,' Adley said thickly. 'You've got plenty of men and guns to do it.'

'I mean legally.'

Adley seemed to consider that a moment. 'Ain't nothing legal about guns. And that's the only way you can move them.'

Stormy had heard enough. With Jim Taylor building a store right in the center of Bluestem and no way to get Ward's homesteaders to move, it meant trouble for Verdune and the Flying V Bar, for Verdune would surely hold that grass north of the creek at any cost.

She went outside, crossed the yard, and caught her horse out of the corral. She wanted a chance to think this through. As she had expected, Jim Taylor was going to be the thorn in the flesh of the Flying V Bar. Verdune had missed more than he realized when he failed to keep Jim on the ranch.

She saddled her horse and rode out of the yard, aiming northeast toward the creek and town. Her course had little conscious direction and she scarcely realized where she was going until her horse slowed to a snail's pace on the trail overlooking Sam Dekin's dugout.

She reined up, looking down on the dugout

58

and recalling the scheme that involved Dekin and a half-dozen other worthless, has-been riders. They were all on Verdune's payroll but their only job was to file homestead papers on a quarter of land along the creek, build a dugout, and prove up on the land. After they had had their papers on the land a year, Verdune was to give them enough money to pay out on their homesteads; then they were to sign the land over to him.

None of the men had a square quarter. Most of them had taken forty-acre blocks that frequently touched only at the corners. Always they had made sure they had included all the creek in their land.

Thinking about it now, Stormy couldn't see what was to keep some of the men from holding the land they had proved up on. Sam Dekin, for instance, was not above such a double-cross. Dekin was a big man, physically capable of hard work but never possessed with the desire. Verdune surely had something to counter such an eventuality. Probably it was the gun that Steve Shane handled so well.

A flurry of activity along the creek to her left caught her eye. Dekin was down there, his rifle in the crook of his arm. And there were two men with a team and heavy wagon facing him.

Nudging her horse, she reined down the slope toward the three men. She got within fifty yards and stopped. She had recognized Jim Taylor as one of the men with the wagon. The man with him was an old fellow with a white beard. His high-pitched voice was railing into Dekin now.

'By Henry, you ain't no part of a homesteader or you'd let us have some sod. We'll pay you for it.'

'You won't pay me,' Sam Dekin rumbled. ''Cause the only way you'll get this sod is over my dead body.'

'You ornery, wobble-jawed sidewinder!' the old man roared. 'I sure hate to have to call you one of my neighbors.'

'I ain't keeping you from moving on,' Dekin retorted.

'Is it Verdune's orders to keep us from getting this creek bottom sod?' Jim asked.

'What's Verdune got to do with it?' Dekin asked sullenly.

'That's what I'd like to know,' Jim said. 'I know he doesn't want any homesteaders on this side of town. And you're no homesteader. You're just a hired stick, proving up on the land for somebody else, probably Verdune.'

'That's a lie!' Dekin snapped. 'I'm homesteading this land for myself.'

Jim took two swift steps forward and grabbed Dekin by his tattered vest. 'Be careful who you're calling a liar, Dekin. I'm not blind. You're no farmer. And you don't have any other way of making a living. Somebody's paying you.'

'Keep your filthy hands off me,' Dekin

60

shouted, and brought the rifle barrel up like a club.

Jim grabbed the rifle with one hand and wrenched, jerking the weapon out of Dekin's grasp. He threw it aside; then, as Dekin made a dive for it, he caught the big fellow's shoulder and gave him a hard shove backward. Dekin stumbled, tried to catch his balance and, failing, tottered a second on the bank of the creek, then splashed into the water with a shrill curse.

The old man ran to the bank and looked over where Dekin was floundering to his feet in the six-inch water. 'Stay in there a while, you bushy-tailed polecat!' he shouted. 'Maybe that water will wash some of the stink off you.'

'Come on, Gramp,' Jim said. 'A hog's a hog and wallowing in the mud won't clean him up.'

Stormy thought she was going to escape detection, sitting still as she was now. But Jim saw her as he turned toward the wagon. He stopped, ignoring Dekin who was climbing out of the creek, dripping and cursing.

'Come on down and join the party,' he invited.

Stormy rode down, looking at Sam Dekin and holding back her laughter with difficulty. 'I'm afraid I'm not prepared for a party.'

'That old goat wasn't either,' Gramp said. 'But he enjoyed it anyway.'

In spite of Stormy's presence, Dekin broke out with a new volley of curses and made a dash for his rifle. Involuntarily, Stormy screamed a warning. 'Look out, Jim.'

'He doesn't want that rifle,' Jim said.

Stormy, watching Dekin, saw him stop suddenly just a couple of steps from the weapon. She whirled to Jim, who had his gun in his hand.

'Just leave the rifle where it is till we're gone, Dekin,' Jim directed. 'It won't rust in that short time. In fact, I think this party would be better off without you. We won't plow up any of your sod.'

Dekin turned toward his dugout, muttering under his breath but being careful to keep his voice low enough not to be understood.

Stormy looked at the plow in the wagon. 'Can't you get sod up on your own land?'

'Looks like we'll have to,' Gramp said. 'But the only sod up there that's any good for houses is what we can plow out of lagoons. Buffalo sod don't hang together as good as this bluestem sod.'

'You may have trouble getting bluestem sod. The creek is settled all the way up.'

Jim nodded. 'We know. And by men like Dekin who get their orders from the same place. Keeping us from plowing sod here wasn't Dekin's idea.'

Anger stirred in Stormy at the backhanded slap aimed at Claude Verdune. 'You treated him as though you blamed him.'

'I wasn't much stuck on his way of telling us

he wouldn't sell.'

'Do you treat everybody who disagrees with you like that?'

Jim grinned. 'Not always. If I did, I'm afraid I'd have to toss you in the creek. And I wouldn't want to do that.'

'I wouldn't advise you to try it,' Stormy said spiritedly.

'I've done things before that you advised me not to try.'

Stormy leaned over the horn of her saddle. 'Aren't you sorry for that yet?'

'Why should I be? I remember it as sort of nice.'

Stormy drummed a fist against her saddle horn. What did it take to put this Jim Taylor in his place? She had had better than average luck in handling men both in college and on the ranch. But here was one who defied all the rules and threw out a challenge she couldn't ignore.

Gramp, who had been watching them, cleared his throat and ran a finger over his bearded chin. 'Say, Jim, we'd better rattle our hocks. Dekin might have another rifle in his dugout, and I've got enough holes in my head without him drilling another one.'

'You're right, Gramp. We're trespassing, I guess.' Jim looked at Stormy and grinned. 'Drop in at my store sometime.'

'I might do that,' Stormy said. 'With a hundred pounds of dynamite.'

Jim and Gramp were in the wagon and Gramp flipped the lines. Stormy watched them go, then reined back up the slope, angling leisurely toward the Flying V Bar.

CHAPTER SIX

In mid-afternoon of the day Jim announced his decision to stock his store, Gramp and two of his neighbors drove their heavy wagons into town. They turned in behind the livery barn that was just going up, and Gramp left the care of his team to the others and cut across to Jim's store.

'Got your order made out?' Gramp asked, surveying the inside of the building which would hold out the weather but otherwise only faintly resembled a store.

'Sure,' Jim said. 'But I wasn't looking for you till morning.'

'We figure on getting an early start. Quite a ways to Big Springs. Ought to make it back in three days if we don't fool around. Time counts this season of the year.'

'Can you spare three days from your farming?'

'No,' Gramp said quickly. 'But getting this store going is about as important to us as our farming. Wes will do what has to be done on my place. The boys and me thought we might bunk here in your store tonight.'

'That will be fine. I'm fixing up the back of the store for living quarters for myself. We can all sleep there.'

'Good.' Gramp looked out into the street where a rider had appeared. 'I figured Betty would follow us,' he said, looking back at Jim, his eyes twinkling. 'Well, three's a crowd. Anyway, I told the boys I'd meet them in a few minutes and we'd see the town.'

Jim grinned. 'Not much to see.'

'The drug store is a mighty interesting place,' Gramp said, and went out.

Jim watched him move down the street, his springy stride belying his seventy years. Then he turned to see Betty swinging down at the new hitchrack Jim had just put in front of his store. The wide-brimmed hat she wore shadowed but didn't hide the perfection of her features. She came in the store, eyes wide in appreciation of the progress of the work. Jim was conscious that today she noticed the store before him, and somehow that pleased him. The store was of prime importance now both to him and the homesteaders. There would be time for other things later.

'You're starting on the shelves, I see,' she said. 'Gramp said you'd be doing business before the week is out. I'm so glad, Jim.'

'Should have my grand opening Saturday if nothing happens to keep Gramp and the boys from getting here with my supplies.'

'This will mean a lot to us. Surely nothing

will happen.'

Jim's face was sober. 'It means a lot to Claude Verdune, too. He doesn't want this store here, remember.'

She nodded. 'I know. But he hasn't interfered yet.'

'I've heard that some animals will stalk their prey for hours in order to get a chance to strike and kill in one blow.'

Betty nodded solemnly, then suddenly smiled. 'I had a little paint left over,' she said gayly. 'Gramp made fun of me for wanting to paint some of your furniture, but I think you'd like that little cabinet better if it had a coat of paint.'

'Probably would,' Jim agreed, as he watched her carefully lift a little can out of her jacket pocket and inspect it to make sure the lid had stayed on tight.

'Won't take me long,' she said, and went through the partition door.

Jim went back to his shelf making, hearing nothing above the steady pounding of his hammer. He wasn't aware that he had more company until a voice cut into a lull in his hammering.

'What does a person have to do here to get some service?'

Jim wheeled, almost dropping his hammer. He had recognized that voice instantly, even though it was about the last voice he expected to hear in his store. Stormy Verdune was

66

standing behind him, laughing at his surprise.

'There isn't much service to be had yet,' Jim said.

'Are you too busy to talk to a future customer?'

'I'm never that busy.' He grinned and laid down his hammer. 'But I hardly expected you to be a customer.'

'You never know what to expect from me.'

Thinking how true that was, he said, 'I suppose you brought that hundred pounds of dynamite?'

'My horse wouldn't carry it,' she said quickly. 'I'll be coming in a wagon some day.'

'Maybe I can sell you some matches then. But if you're going to be a customer, it seems we ought to be on a little friendlier footing.'

'We're on speaking terms. Isn't that enough for a customer?'

'Maybe. But why do we have to be enemies?'

She ran a finger over a newly made counter. 'Let's say we're friendly enemies. We're on opposite sides of the fence and it doesn't look like either of us will be climbing over.'

'Just how do friendly enemies act, say, at the Saturday night shindig?'

'They dance together, of course; at least once.'

He grinned. 'Can I count on that?'

'I give you my word, even if we're shooting at each other before the music stops.'

He laughed, and she joined in. 'We have to

check our guns, remember,' he reminded her.

Jim had forgotten Betty for a moment and he didn't hear the partition door open, but he felt her presence before she spoke. Stormy looked toward the back of the store.

'A customer, Jim?'

The way Betty said it was a slap in the face both to Stormy and Jim. It was funny, he thought, how much venom a woman could put into a simple statement. And Stormy, a tomboyish rogue a moment before, was suddenly a sharp-tongued female with a viper's sting in her words.

'At least this customer is not in the back room.'

Betty colored. 'Come back and let me show you what I'm painting. In fact, I'll rub your face in it.'

'Hold on now,' Jim said sharply. 'Let the men do any fighting that's got to be done. I sure don't figure on getting my new store torn up in a hairpulling contest.'

Both girls looked at him, and finally Stormy laughed. 'It's your store, Jim. There'll be better ways of getting it torn up than this. I'll see you around.'

She went out and Betty watched her until she had passed from the range of her vision. Then she turned to Jim.

'Why did she come in here?'

Jim shrugged. 'I don't know. Curiosity, I guess. Calls herself a friendly enemy.'

68

Betty's lips formed a straight hard line. 'Friendly! She was in here to spy for her father. Verdune probably wants to know how soon you'll be ready to open the store.'

'She didn't ask.'

'Of course not. But she's not blind. She could see.'

Jim laughed to ease the tension.

But before he could reply, the door opened and the two young homesteaders who had come into town with Gramp stumbled in. Big bruises showed purple on their cheeks and eyes, and one wiped blood from his nose as he leaned against a new counter.

'What happened to you?' Jim demanded.

Betty ran past him. 'Did you have a fight, Hank?'

The man called Hank frowned and looked at the floor. 'You can't fight with a gun in your back. We can't haul for you, Jim.'

Jim nodded grimly. 'So that's how it is. Somebody beats you up and makes you promise not to haul my supplies.'

Hank nodded. 'It ain't what we want to do. But hauling for you is unhealthy business. We were told that this was just a sample of what we'd get if we did haul.'

'Who made that threat?'

'Harder was the big finger. He had a couple of gun slicks with him. One of them held a gun on us while Harder beat us up. We didn't have a chance to fight back.'

69

'That's the way Verdune will do his fighting,' Betty said, anger burning high in her cheeks. 'I wish I were a man!'

'Wouldn't do you no good unless you were mighty fast with a gun,' Hank said. 'We ain't.'

'Where's Gramp?' Jim asked suddenly.

'He was still down in the drug store when we left. They hadn't bothered him.'

'They will,' Betty screamed. 'You've got to get him out of there, Jim.'

But Jim was already running toward the back of the store where he had his things. It took him but a second to get his gun belt. He made it a point to keep it where it would be handy. And he knew the gun was loaded and in working order. Those inspections were daily chores with him now. He buckled the belt around his waist as he ran back through the store.

'Better be careful,' Hank warned. 'There are three of them and they know how to handle guns.'

'Gramp doesn't,' Jim reminded them, disgust in his voice. Maybe he shouldn't criticize the two homesteaders. They weren't fighting men. Still, they had left Gramp alone at the mercy of three gunmen.

'Be careful, Jim,' Betty called as he went through the door.

The drug store was just on the other side of the Verdune House, and it took Jim only a few seconds to reach the front of it. He went in and headed for the partition door in the back. He
70

heard a curse and a pop as a fist slapped against flesh. Then came Gramp's high-pitched voice, the words blistering in their denunciation of Harder and his gunnies. Jim had his gun in his hand when he kicked open the partition door.

Activity in the little room stopped when Jim burst in. Gramp was backed against the far wall and Harder was standing over him, fists knotted. One of the two men Hank had said were with Harder was close to him now, apparently enjoying the beating Gramp was taking. Jim didn't see the other man. But before he could look over the rest of the room, he heard him.

'Let your gun drop easy, Taylor,' the man said directly behind Jim.

Jim had no choice as he felt the prodding point of a gun in his back. Harder grinned triumphantly, and as Gramp started to slip away from him, he grabbed his shirt front and slammed him back against the wall.

'Maybe we can convince Taylor that he ain't supposed to haul any stuff in here if he sees us work the old man over,' Harder said, anticipation in his face.

'I won't promise nothing,' Gramp shouted.

Harder hit him across the mouth and blood trickled down over the stained whiskers. Jim held himself back with an effort. Harder struck again and Gramp sagged back against the wall.

'When you agree not to do that freighting,

we'll let you go,' Harder said, and hit the old man again. Every muscle tight, he suddenly jabbed an elbow straight back, twisting away as he struck. His elbow buried itself in the man's soft stomach and the breath exploded from him. Surprise kept him from using the gun for an instant. And that instant was all that Jim needed.

Whirling, he caught the wrist behind the gun and twisted sharply. Before the other men realized what was happening, Jim had the gun wrenched out of the man's grasp. As it clattered to the floor, Harder wheeled and lunged toward Jim. Jim met the challenge, ignoring the man he had just disarmed. Out of the tail of his eye he saw Gramp erupt into action, scooping up the gun and covering Harder's two henchmen.

Jim caught Harder with a straight left jab that rocked the big man back on his heels. Gramp's shrill voice cut in then.

'Get back with those other yellow pups, Harder.'

'Let him alone, Gramp,' Jim said, his anger white hot. 'Keep the other two out. I want Harder for myself.'

'You've got him,' Gramp yelled gleefully. 'Beat him to death.'

Harder sneered and moved forward confidently, a big man with a bull neck and powerful arms and shoulders. Jim threw a straight jab that landed with a solid jolt on the

72

point of Harder's nose. Blood squirted over the big man's face and he roared like a wounded lion. Jim backed away quickly, knowing he wouldn't get another chance like that but satisfied that he had done some real damage.

Harder circled warily, then suddenly dodged in, trying to get close with those murderously powerful arms. But Jim had expected such a move and kept out of his reach. He landed two more quick jabs on that nose. The first blow, he guessed, had broken Harder's nose, judging from the twisted, mashed look it had.

Harder cursed when the jabs hit and bore in with renewed fury. His fist caught Jim in the ribs and twisted him back to the wall. But Jim shoved away before Harder could close in. Gasping for breath, he backpedaled as Harder wheeled after him, eagerness firing his eyes. Jim dimmed that eager light with a shot over the big fellow's guard that mashed the pulpy nose again. Harder's uncontrolled howl of pain rocked the room. Gramp cheered gleefully, but he didn't make the mistake of relaxing his guard over the other two men.

Harder came forward again, but his guard was higher now, protecting his nose. Jim took a sharp blow on the ear that made his head ring, then lowered his aim and buried a fist just under Harder's ribs. Breath exploded from the bully and he leaned forward, his guard dropping.

Jim whipped both fists to the swelling nose

in rapid succession. Harder reeled backward with an agonizing groan. Jim followed him, alternating his blows between the midriff and the nose.

By the time Harder had backed to the wall, he had given up. His nose was a bloody smear on his face and one eye was beginning to close.

'Had enough?' Jim demanded when Harder dropped his guard helplessly.

'Enough,' Harder panted through swelling lips.

Jim turned to Gramp and took his gun. 'I want this understood, Harder,' he said before stepping through the partition door. 'When these men haul my supplies, I'm holding you personally responsible for anything that happens to them. If they are bothered, you'll think what just happened to you was a picnic. Is that clear?'

Harder nodded but said nothing. Nichols, the owner of the drug store, came in through the back door. Surprise washed over his face as he took in the scene. Jim guessed that he had gone out so he couldn't be held responsible for what happened.

Beckoning for Gramp to follow, Jim led the way back to his own store.

CHAPTER SEVEN

May slipped away and Jim found the supplies he had brought in from Big Springs dwindling.

74

There had been no trouble and Jim entertained brief moments of hope that Verdune would let him alone. But he knew in those moments he was living in a fool's paradise. Verdune hadn't really begun to fight. His ambitions were high; he wouldn't give up those ambitions until he was thoroughly licked.

Stormy came into town one morning and stopped at Jim's store. This morning she had not ridden a horse but had brought a light surrey.

'Anything I can sell you this morning?' he asked.

'Just a little time killer,' she said. 'When does the hack get in?'

'It's supposed to pull in about ten but generally it's ten minutes to an hour late. Leaves Sagehorn early, goes back from here right after dinner. Runs every other day.'

'I know its history and schedule. I just wanted to know when it really got in. If it's on time, I've got half an hour to wait.'

'Must be somebody special coming in on the hack,' Jim ventured.

'Special for some. Not for you.'

The stage rolled in on time and Stormy hurried out to the Verdune House where it stopped. A tall, neatly dressed man got off the hack and greeted Stormy with a warmth that hinted at more than a casual acquaintance. He held his hat in his hand and his well groomed

75

blond hair glistened in the sunlight. Jim judged him to be in the neighborhood of thirty.

A slow fire kindled in Jim as he watched the newcomer guide Stormy possessively up the steps of the Verdune House. Something about the oily smooth manner of the man struck a discordant note in Jim.

Jim went back to his shelves, arranging the goods and wishing there were more supplies to display. He kept one eye on the street, watching for Stormy and the blond man to leave, for he figured that the new man was heading for the Flying V Bar. But instead of the surrey leaving town, a rider came in and reined up at the Verdune House.

Jim left his work and went to the window to watch Claude Verdune go up the steps. Before he left the window, he saw Tom Biggs cross from his store to the hotel. Then Nichols, the druggist, and Eddie Lowe came down the street and went in after Biggs.

Jim turned back to his work but his mind stayed on the hotel. The new man must be somebody of importance in Verdune's scheme of things to warrant a meeting of Verdune's stooges the minute he hit town.

Jim waited impatiently until the meeting broke up and the merchants went back to their stores. He saw Verdune come out and ride down the street without looking to right or left. Then Stormy and the blond man came out more leisurely and got in the surrey, talking and laughing.

When they were out of town and the street had returned to its normal emptiness, Jim left his store and went down to the office of the Bluestem Bugle. Curiosity was nagging at him, and Eddie Lowe was the only man who had been at that meeting who would tell him anything.

Lowe was busy writing at his desk when Jim came in. He glanced up, and a startled look crossed his face.

'Got something to put in your paper, Eddie?' Jim asked.

Lowe nodded. 'A lot.'

'Something that can't be told until publication?'

'It's no secret. Bluestem is being organized.'

Jim nodded. He wasn't surprised; still it dealt him a solid jolt. He knew what organization would do for him, an outcast in a town banded together by one law, Verdune's. 'I suppose that new sandy-haired fellow had something to do with that,' he said.

Lowe nodded. 'He talked like it was his idea, but I reckon it wasn't. I've been hearing talk about organizing this town since I first got here.'

'Who is this new man?'

'Fellow named Chester Fyfe. He's a lawyer. Stormy got acquainted with him when she was going to school back East. Claims to be quite a politician. He's out here to manage Verdune's

77

campaign.'

'What does Verdune need with a campaign manager?' Jim asked. 'He doesn't have any opposition in the primaries.'

'He will have in the general election in November. Fyfe claims it's necessary to plan far ahead. He made it sound convincing. He's got a smooth tongue.'

'He's smooth all over, I'd say,' Jim said, thinking of the impression Fyfe had made on him. 'I suppose you're going to have officers for the town?'

'Sure,' Lowe said, glancing back at the paper he was working on. 'We'll have an election of town officials the same day as the primary election. The polls for the state primaries will be in the town hall. The town election will be held in the back of Biggs' store.'

Jim nodded. Lowe had been a good source of information. He started for the door. 'They'll have to get their candidates lined up pretty quick,' he said, 'or will there be just one candidate for each office?'

Lowe shifted uncomfortably. 'They've got the nominations all made. Your name is up for mayor.'

Surprise hit Jim hard. 'Why do they went me on the ballot?'

'I don't ask questions,' Lowe said. 'There are two names for every office. Verdune says people ought to have a choice. Tom Biggs is running against you.'

78

'That will be some race,' Jim said disgustedly, and went outside.

He couldn't see why Verdune had put his name on the ballot unless it was an attempt to humiliate him. Nobody under Verdune's thumb would dare vote for him. And everyone in town except Jim was either directly or indirectly under the rancher's thumb . . . .

June came, and with it election day. Jim had given it little thought. There were no really interesting contests on the primary ballot, and the town ballot offered no contests at all with any meaning.

Jim's store hadn't been open an hour when Steve Shane came in and immediately showed signs of settling on the counter for the day. He rolled a smoke, hitched himself into a more comfortable position where he could see both the town hall and Biggs' store through the window, and relaxed.

'It's going to be a long day, Steve,' Jim said pointedly. 'Why did Verdune send you in?'

'To see that everything stayed peaceable. Wouldn't do for a candidate to have trouble at the polls in his own precinct.'

Jim nodded. 'I reckon not. Must be tough being a politician.'

'You ought to know. I hear you're running for mayor of this fair city.'

Jim grinned. 'You hear a lot of things. I'm not running. I'm being pushed. They just needed another name on the ballot. I'm afraid

79

I'd make a pretty poor politician.'

'Verdune says he's a statesman, not a politician. He thinks the word politician is degrading.'

'The shoe doesn't pinch unless it fits pretty tight,' Jim said. 'Dad used to say the difference between a politician and a statesman is that a politician looks ahead to the next election while a statesman looks ahead to the next generation. According to that, I'd say Verdune is a politician whether he likes the word or not.'

Steve, staring absently out the window, didn't seem to hear. Jim watched, analyzing his old partner.

'Has that new fellow, Fyfe, cut you out?' he asked finally.

Steve started as if Jim had slappped him. 'Who said anything about Fyfe?'

'I did,' Jim said. 'I've seen you down in the dumps before. Usually over some girl. I figure Stormy has given you the mitten to run around with that lawyer.'

Steve's face clouded. 'That puffed-up windbag! I bet I could lick him with one hand tied behind my back.'

'I won't take that bet,' Jim said. 'Looks like we're both playing second fiddle, Steve. You to that lawyer, Fyfe, and me to Verdune's whole layout here in town. Let's go over and vote.'

'Nobody to vote for but Verdune as far as I'm concerned, and he ain't got anybody running against him. I'll go with you, though, and scratch a ballot.'

They crossed to the town hall and drew a ballot apiece. Sitting down at a convenient table, they marked the ballots and turned them in. Only a few people were at the hall and most of them seemed to be hanging around just to see how people voted.

Outside again, Steve nodded toward Biggs' store. 'Better go in and vote for mayor.'

'There's nobody running for mayor that I want to have the job,' Jim said.

The day wore away, Steve keeping his position close to the window where he could watch the street. He stayed with Jim until the polls closed. Then he went over to Biggs' store. Jim got his store ready to close, then waited, for he knew Steve would be back. When he came, Jim met him at the front door.

'You're more popular than you thought you were,' Steve said. 'You got one vote for mayor.'

'Who would vote for me?' Jim asked.

'I can't figure out unless you voted before I got to town.'

'I didn't. I suppose Harder got the marshal job.'

Steve nodded. 'Sure. And Biggs is mayor. But I'd like to know who voted for you. Verdune will want to know that, too.'

'Think he'll find out?'

'Probably. But it won't make much difference. Just somebody in the ranks who got out of step. He'll get back in.'

Steve mounted his horse and left town. Jim watched him go, but he wasn't thinking about Steve or even the one vote that had been cast for him. With Tom Biggs as mayor and Ross Harder as marshal, life in Bluestem was going to be tough for Jim.

CHAPTER EIGHT

Jim didn't see Gramp or Betty for several days. Then they drove into town just before sundown and stopped in front of his store. Excitement brightened the old man's eyes and put spring in Betty's step as she bounced out of the buggy and across the porch into the store.

'You look like a kid who has just found where the cookie jar is hidden,' Jim said. 'Where have you been?'

'To McCook among other places. We've been visiting the settlers along the creek this afternoon.' Excitement ran high in her voice. 'We're having a meeting at our place tonight. You've got to come, Jim.'

'What's the meeting about?'

'We'll tell you when you get there.'

'And by Henry,' Gramp said from the doorway, 'you'd better show up, or I'll come in and drag you out there by your whiskers.'

Jim didn't hurry out to Ward's place after he finished supper. All day he had seen men with teams and scrapers working down along the

82

creek bank. Curiosity directed his steps that way. He had heard talk of a flour mill to be built and a dam across the creek to furnish water power to run the mill.

The dirt piled out in a rough dike back several yards on either side of the stream left no doubt that what he had heard was correct. Jim thought of the fishing that could be had when the dam was filled. There were suckers, chubs, and sunfish in the creek now, and likely the dam would be stocked with other fish.

He went back to the barn and got his horse, his mind returning to the promise of a surprise out at Ward's tonight.

The yard in front of Wes Ward's soddy was packed with rigs and saddled horses. Half the homesteaders in the west end of Verdune County was here, Jim guessed.

He found a place for his horse at a corral post and went into the house. He recognized most of the faces. All of Ward's outfit was here and a good representation of the homesteaders downstream from Bluestem.

It seemed to Jim that every eye turned on him when he came in. He tried to slip through to the kitchen where he could corner Betty and make her tell him something about the meeting, but the crowd pressed in on him. Before he could work his way across the room, Gramp climbed up on a chair and waved a hand for silence. A hush fell on the men and eyes turned from Jim to Gramp.

'Jim's finally got here,' the old man announced, 'so we can get on with our meeting. Everybody get a seat that can find one and the rest of you stand some place where you won't be in the way.'

The men shuffled around, and one man that Jim had overlooked came into view. He was a big man, six feet tall and weighing at least two hundred and fifty pounds. Jim guessed that most of the bulk was flabby fat rather than hard muscle. He wore a well pressed dark suit and his cheeks were as ruddy as if he had just run a hundred yards. His sharp black eyes darted over the room as the shuffling gradually subsided.

'Now then,' Gramp said when things were quiet, 'probably all of you but Jim know why we're holding this meeting. But we've got to do this official. And Mr. Ostrand here is just the man to see that it gets done that way.'

Gramp hopped down from the chair. Ostrand looked at the chair, gave it a test shake with his two hundred and fifty pounds, then decided in favor of remaining on the floor.

'As Mr. Shepherd said,' Ostrand began in a steady carrying voice that marked him as a man used to public speaking, 'most of you know the purpose of this meeting. For those of you who don't, I'll state it briefly.'

Jim tabbed the man as one who had no inkling of what the word brief meant. Ostrand filled the picture Jim carried of the long-winded speakers who held sway at Fourth of July and Decoration Day celebrations.

'We're here,' Ostrand went on clearly, 'because of the deplorable fact that John Kelley has seen fit to withdraw his name from the legislative race. I know that most of you are not pleased with the prospect of having Claude Verdune railroaded into office. He would not be a fair representative of the people of this district.'

It seemed to Jim that every man in the room was hanging on Ostrand's words. Somebody shouted, 'Why did Kelley back out?'

'I don't know for certain,' Ostrand said, 'and I do not feel free to voice my opinions. But his withdrawal came under strange circumstances. That isn't important now. The fact is, we're without a suitable candidate to oppose Verdune. It is our purpose to get one.'

A cheer rocked the room, but Jim, trying to fathom Ostrand's meaning, didn't join in. After a minute, Ostrand held up his hand.

'I'm proposing that we circulate a petition to put Jim Taylor's name on the ballot with Verdune in this fall's election.'

The roar that greeted this statement was deafening.

'What do you say, Jim?' Gramp asked excitedly, tugging at Jim's arm.

'Nothing doing,' Jim said without hesitation.

The excitement drained out of Gramp's face and the noise in the room subsided to a murmur. Jim saw the disappointment in the faces of the homesteaders. But it didn't change his decision.

Ostrand cut smoothly into the silence. 'Just a minute. I don't think Mr. Taylor fully appreciates what we're asking. He hasn't had time to consider it.'

'I'm no politician.'

'That's one of your greatest assets,' Ostrand said quickly. 'We've got too many politicians in Lincoln now. We need honest representatives down there, men who know the needs of the people and are willing to fight for those needs. We want a man who isn't after the almighty dollar, who isn't trying to pull all the strings to get reelected. We've decided you're that man.'

Jim fumbled for an answer. All the elements of surprise were being used against him. He had never pictured himself as a candidate for any office and he couldn't quite grasp it now. The impression he had always carried of a politician was not one he wanted associated with himself.

'You don't want Verdune for our representative, do you?' Gramp demanded.

'No more than you do,' Jim admitted. 'But I don't know enough about politics to campaign against Verdune. And I probably wouldn't know how to do my duty in Lincoln if I should get there.'

'Let us worry about the campaign,' Ostrand said quickly. 'As for doing your duty once you

86

are elected, that is no problem. All that the people of this district want is honest representation, a man who will go down to Lincoln and tell them what the folk out here in this western end of the state need and then vote for the things that will help these people. Don't tell me you can't do that.'

Again Jim couldn't find an answer to the direct challenge.

'What can I do in Lincoln that Verdune wouldn't do?' he asked, postponing a definite decision for another minute.

'Giving the settlers a square deal,' Ostrand said. 'I happen to know that one of the things Verdune intends to place before the legislature is a bill to restrict the herd law to the eastern part of the state. The people back there think the western end of the state is a wilderness and not fit for farming. With the influence Verdune has built up during his previous terms as a representative from an eastern district, he can get that bill through. Without the protection of the herd law, the homesteaders can't keep Verdune's cattle from running over their crops. It will mean the end of homesteading out here, and Verdune and men like him will soon have complete control of this entire country.'

The faces of the men around Ostrand told Jim plainly that this wasn't the first they had heard of Verdune's scheme. Men crowded around Jim as Ostrand laid a hand on his shoulder. 'Please say that you're willing to be our standard bearer.'

'If you get enough names on the petitions to have my name printed on the ballot, I'll do my best,' Jim capitulated.

'That's good enough,' Ostrand boomed, clapping Jim on the back. 'Getting the signers is merely a matter of circulating the petitions. Every man here will sign and a lot have already signed at Sand Creek. I'll put men to work in every part of the district. Within a week, we'll have the signatures of a large enough percentage of the voters to get your name on the ballot with Verdune.'

The men took turns affixing their signatures to the petition Ostrand produced. Then they left the house, after pledging Jim their personal support. As Jim rode out of the yard, his eyes turned involuntarily to stare into the darkness toward the Flying V Bar. He had been a thorn in Claude Verdune's side before, but now he was striking at the very heart of the man's pride. Verdune wouldn't take it lying down.

CHAPTER NINE

The news of the meeting at Ward's traveled on the wings of the wind.

Just before noon the next day, a horse slid to a dusty stop in front of the store. Jim glanced at the rider and braced himself.

Stormy Verdune hadn't brought Chester

Fyfe with her this morning. She had come alone, and her mission was apparent even before she leaped angrily from her saddle.

'Well, you've done it, haven't you?' she snapped, coming to a halt at the counter three feet from him.

'That's according,' he said slowly, thinking that time would calm her more than anything he could say. 'I've done lots of things in my time.'

'This tops anything you could ever have done,' she retorted. 'Just what do you think you'll gain by running for the legislature?'

'They tell me I might gain a job down in Lincoln,' he said with more confidence than he felt.

'A fat chance you've got! What do you know about politics?'

'Not much,' he admitted.

'You're due to learn plenty before election this fall. Dad has been in politics for years, and what he doesn't know about it, Chester does. Between them, they'll make a monkey out of you.'

Jim said nothing. Stormy slapped the quirt which dangled from her wrist against the calf of her leg.

'Well?' she demanded. 'Aren't you going to say anything?'

He grinned. 'I thought you'd already said it. We'll just wait and see how much of a monkey I am.'

She wheeled toward the door. 'When the votes are in this fall, you won't know you've been in an election except for the people laughing at you.'

She went through the door, slamming it behind her. Jim looked after her, wondering if she might not be a good prophet.

He went to the window and looked idly along the street. Down close to the river a team and scraper was going along the bank, heading for the dam a hundred yards upstream. Jim had heard that they expected to have the dam done and full of water by the Fourth of July.

The day came for the Bluestem *Bugle* to make its weekly appearance. Jim had been waiting for the paper to see what it would say about him. He was watching the *Bugle* office for Lowe to take his papers across to the post office when Gramp rode into town. Gramp was slumped in his saddle, his face squinted and drawn from weariness, but there was an air of triumph about his stride when he swung down and came into the store.

'Been down to Sand Creek,' Gramp announced importantly. 'Just got back this morning. Saw Ostrand. He said to tell you he has enough signers now to get your name on the ballot.'

'What good will that do?' Jim asked listlessly. 'I won't have a ghost of a chance against Verdune.'

'You listen to me,' Gramp said sternly.

'Ostrand said for you to get a spot on the Fourth of July program. A speech then will get you in the public eye and start your campaign rolling.'

Jim stared at Gramp. 'Verdune is the main speaker on that program. They wouldn't let me speak if I wanted to.'

'You want to and you're going to,' Gramp said firmly. 'You ain't going to take votes from Verdune by running from him. You've got to beat him at his own game—talking.'

'I'm no orator. Verdune would make me look like a fool.'

'Ostrand says you've got to get on that program. There'll be people here for that celebration that won't see another candidate before election, and they won't read a word of stuff you send them. It's your only chance to get to those people.'

Ostrand knew his politics, Jim admitted. But he didn't know his candidate. 'I can't talk against Verdune,' Jim said flatly. 'What would I say?'

'Ostrand says to keep your speech simple. Just tell the folks exactly why you're running against that land hog.'

'Nothing doing,' Jim said after another minute's consideration. 'I'll get more votes by keeping my mouth shut.'

'Nobody ever won a race backing up,' Gramp said hotly, and stormed out the door.

Through the store window, Jim saw Eddie

91

Lowe crossing the street with a bundle of papers. He left the store and cut across to the post office. Lowe was just leaving when Jim got to the door. Jim spoke, but Lowe dropped his eyes, mumbling an incoherent greeting. Jim frowned and went on inside. Lowe was generally friendly. There must be a reason behind the editor's sudden change, and Jim had a feeling he'd find that reason when he got his paper.

As soon as the postmaster finished distributing the papers, Jim got his from his box. The big headline caught his eye instantly.

'BIG SWINDLE ATTEMPTED' the headline read. Below in smaller type was the warning: 'Uneducated for the job; unfit for the job.'

Jim didn't need to read farther. But he did. 'That describes the candidate who is opposing the very able Claude Verdune in the race for the legislature. Jim Taylor, who has absolutely no political knowledge, who probably wouldn't know a bill from a law, is asking the people of this district to send him to Lincoln to represent them. It is an insult to the intelligence of the fine people of our district. It takes years of special study and training to become a good representative, one who will vote for the measures that will do his people the most good. How does Taylor fit that pattern?'

There was more, but Jim had read enough. The Bluestem *Bugle* was the only source of information many of the settlers had, and this editorial would do much toward killing any budding support for his campaign.

Folding the paper, he crossed the street to the office of the *Bugle*. He'd better find out right now just where he stood with Lowe. His chances of staying in the race against Verdune would be mighty slim if the paper continued printing such editorials as this one.

Lowe was at his desk when Jim came through the door. The editor looked up, the surprise and fear on his small baby-like face reminding Jim of a startled bird.

'Something I can do for you?' he asked uneasily.

'There certainly is.' Jim found a stool across the desk from Lowe and perched himself on it. 'I don't like your editorial, Eddie.'

Lowe looked down at the papers before him. 'I didn't expect you to.'

'What have I done to make you think so highly of me?' Jim asked, an edge to his words.

'Nothing, Jim. It's just—'

'Verdune's orders?'

Lowe nodded. 'He got me this job.'

'Does that mean he owns you body and soul? Does he tell you every move you can make?'

'That's part of the bargain,' Lowe said miserably.

Jim felt both disgust and pity for the little editor. No bigger than a boy sprouting his first whiskers, he was the picture of dejection as he

93

sat humped over on his desk stool. The editorial hadn't been his idea, but that didn't lessen the damage it would do to Jim's chances with the homesteaders down the creek.

'You don't have to do everything that Verdune says,' Jim said. 'No man is that important.'

'One man is, Jim.' Lowe slipped off his stool and moved restlessly around the little office. 'I'm not a fighter like you. And even if I was, I couldn't buck the odds against me.'

Jim nodded slowly, beginning to glimpse a light he hadn't suspected before. 'Verdune has you on the short end of the stick?'

Lowe nodded. 'Any time he says the word, my name will be mud.'

'Surely it's not that bad.'

'That bad and worse.' Lowe took a turn around the room. 'But my troubles are none of your business.'

'That's right, Eddie. Except I've got good reasons to want you out from under Verdune's thumb.'

'There's no chance of that. I've got to print what Verdune says. I hope you'll understand.'

'It's a little hard to understand when somebody's kicking you in the face,' Jim said slowly.

Lowe's fists were knotted at his sides and beads of perspiration dotted his forehead as he paced back and forth behind his desk. 'You've got to understand, Jim. You're about the only

94

friend I have in town. Sure, there are a lot of us bowing and scraping to Verdune, but none of us has any respect for the other. We're all in the same boat.'

'I'd like to see it your way, Eddie. But I can't imagine any man telling me exactly what I could or couldn't say or do.'

Lowe stopped suddenly in front of Jim. 'You could if that man knew you were wanted for murder.'

Jim felt as if he had been dealt a body blow. 'Not you, Eddie!' he said unbelievingly.

Lowe nodded and sank back on his stool. 'I'm wanted on a charge of murder down in Kansas.'

'And Verdune knows about it?'

'Not only knows about it; he is the one who sprung me out of jail. I had an argument with a man down in Kansas where I was working on a weekly newspaper. This fellow was disliked by almost everybody and a dozen people had reasons to kill him. But he was killed the night after we had our quarrel. It was made to look like I did it. I was brought up on trial and it was all cut and dried. I didn't have the money to get a good lawyer, and somebody had been very careful to have all the evidence handy to convict me.'

Lowe took another turn around the room, looking out into the street as if to make sure no one was near. Then he sat down again and Jim waited, knowing now that he would hear

95

Lowe's whole story.

'The last day of the trial I saw Verdune there. I didn't know him, but his was a new face and I remembered it. Later after I had been sentenced to ninety-nine years in the state penitentiary, Verdune came to the jail to see me. They wouldn't let him talk to me but I saw him in the front office.

'That night after supper I heard a racket up front, and then Verdune came running down the corridor with the keys. He told me there was a lynch mob forming but when he told the sheriff, the sheriff laughed at him. Verdune said he wouldn't let them hang me. He told me he thought I was innocent but I'd never have a chance to prove it down in the pen. Verdune looked like an angel to me that night. I wasn't worrying about the mob. All I could think of was that lifetime stretch.

'Verdune said he wanted me to come to a spot in western Nebraska and run a newspaper for him. I was to change my name, and he assured me nobody would ever find me. It sounded like a good deal so I took it.'

'You didn't have much choice, it seems to me,' Jim said when Lowe stopped for breath.

'I didn't. I had to run. I came here, thinking I could start all over and do the community a service while I was at it. But Verdune had ideas about how this paper should be run. All he needs to do is say the word, and the law will grab me and ship me back to Kansas to spend the rest of my life rotting in prison.'

'I suppose you'll have to print what Verdune says,' Jim said finally. 'We'll hope something happens to change that. If it doesn't, it will mean certain election for him this fall.'

Lowe nodded. 'I'm afraid so. I hate to see Verdune elected worse than you know. But what can I do?'

'You might pull up stakes.'

'I've thought of that. But he's got me blocked there, too. He didn't leave a loophole.'

'How can he keep you from running out?'

'I didn't tell you the name of the man I was supposed to have murdered. It was Sam Harder.'

Jim whistled softly. 'Some relation to Ross Harder?'

'A brother. Ross was in Texas during the trial. He had never seen me until he came to Bluestem. Verdune hasn't admitted it, but I know he brought Harder here. I heard Harder say once that he had been promised if he stayed here long enough he would get some information about his brother's killer. And he has sworn to avenge Sam.'

'Verdune holds two clubs over you then,' Jim said, realizing the spot the editor was in.

Lowe rose to pace the floor again. 'Ross Harder is a killer just like his brother was. I could run away from Verdune, but if I did, Verdune would set Harder on my trail and he'd catch me. As long as I toe the mark, Verdune won't tell Harder I'm the man who was convicted of killing Sam. But I can't draw a breath and say it's my own without asking Verdune.'

Jim rose to leave. 'I'm sorry I said anything about that editorial.'

'I'm not,' Lowe said, and there was a light in his eyes Jim hadn't seen since that first day when he had found Lowe helping build the little newspaper office. 'You know now why I wrote it and why I'll have to write more like it. You've played square with me; I want to do the same with you, and if I get the chance to give you a boost, I'll do it.'

Jim went out into the street. He knew he ought to be burning at the injustice being done to him by the editorial. But he wondered what he would do if he were in Lowe's place.

Betty came to town in the afternoon and got the mail. She stopped at the store, seething with anger.

Jim nodded at the paper she was carrying. 'I've seen it.'

'What are you going to do about it?' she demanded.

'Too late to do much.'

'This will ruin you, Jim,' Betty said, almost in tears.

'It won't help my campaign any,' he admitted. 'But the paper is in the post office now. It can't be taken back.'

'But there may be more editorials like that.

98

You've got to stop them, Jim.'

Jim hesitated, wishing he could tell Betty about Lowe's predicament and knowing he couldn't. 'It's a free press, Betty. We can't keep Lowe from printing anything he likes.'

Anger flashed in her eyes. 'We've got to do something. You can't expect to beat Verdune if you let him get away with this.'

'I know. But it's hard to compete against the only newspaper in the country.'

Betty turned toward the door. 'We'll think of something. Maybe you can find a way to counter this editorial in your speech on the Fourth.'

'They won't let me on that program. I couldn't make a speech, anyway.'

At the door, Betty turned to face Jim. All trace of tears was gone now. She was calm, and there was a thoughtful look in her eyes. 'You'd better get to work on your speech, Jim. You're going to be on that platform the Fourth and you're going to make an appeal to the voters of this district to elect an honest representative to the legislature. And you're going to be that representative.'

Jim mulled the situation over in his mind far into the night. He was still awake when a sound outside the store just on the other side of the wall from his bed brought him up in his blankets.

His hand crept under the pillow to the gun he kept there. He lay motionless until the sound came again. Something or somebody was moving around just outside the store. As he slipped quietly out of bed, he heard a sputtering crackle outside, and it sent a chill trickling down his spine. That was a fire, and its purpose was only too clear to Jim.

Running softly to the back door, he let himself out. He couldn't afford to waste any time, but he wanted to get a look at the firebug. He peeked around the corner of the store in time to see a man dodging into the street at the front of the building, evidently certain that his blaze was well started. Jim took a quick shot at the man and knew he had missed. But the roar of the shot in the quiet night air would wake the whole town.

He turned his attention to putting out the blaze. It was licking hungrily up a pile of kerosene-soaked rags and sticks and had already attacked the wall of the store. He shuddered when he thought what would have happened if he hadn't heard the fire start.

Dashing back into the store, he grabbed his pail of drinking water and brought it out. The one bucketful of water wasn't enough to smother the flames completely, but it put out the heart of the fire and Jim quickly scooped dirt over the remaining embers.

He heard a shout down the street but he didn't answer. He realized suddenly that he wasn't dressed for company and hurried back inside.

He went back to bed but sleep was furtive and tantalizing, always beckoning but never coming near enough to be overtaken. He had no illusions about the motive for setting the blaze. It was unlikely that the man held a personal grudge against Jim. He was Verdune's man. And this was one of Verdune's ways of striking back at Jim for challenging his right to be lord of all around him.

Some of the tension drained out of Jim as he thought of it. Fire and guns were weapons he understood much better than words.

CHAPTER TEN

It was Bluestem's first celebration. The firing of the anvils at sunrise in the traditional morning salute started the day.

It seemed to Jim that everyone within a fifteen mile radius had poured into town by ten o'clock. Buckboards and buggies lined the streets and were standing on vacant lots behind the stores. Several families had driven down close to the dam and had unhitched there. Claude Verdune came late in the surrey, moving in dignity down the crowded street. Jim noted that Chester Fyfe was with Stormy in the back seat, and a new man he had never seen before shared the front with Verdune.

A platform had been built down close to the creek north of the *Bugle* office. Planks laid

101

across nail kegs made rows of seats in front of the platform, and these seats were filled shortly after ten. Tom Biggs was bustling around like an old hen.

The morning portion of the program was short, beginning with the customary reading of the Declaration of Independence. A few numbers followed, but Jim paid little attention; his mind was on the speech he would have to make from that platform this afternoon.

Jim accepted Betty's invitation to eat dinner with the Wards, and they found a spot for their picnic lunch close to the dam where dozens of families were eating. The youngsters in the group closest to the Wards were talking excitedly about the races they were going to be in. Only one race held much interest for Jim. That was the tub race to be staged on the dam. It was for the businessmen of the town, with five dollars going to the winner. Jim hadn't been too eager to enter, but he knew Verdune would make good political use of his refusal to cooperate if he didn't take a hand.

The race was to start two hundred yards upstream from the dam and the first man to beach his tub on the dam would be the winner. Each man had a tub assigned to him, and he was given a pole to guide and push his tub along.

Jim got down to the water's edge and was handed a tub by Verdune, who was the official starter. Jim saw Tom Biggs, out of his role as

102

program chairman, testing the bottom of his tub for leaks. Ross Harder, the marshal, and Nichols, the druggist, were there, and a couple of other businessmen in town. There was one more tub than contestants. Verdune said something to his foreman, Bruce Noble, and Noble disappeared into the crowd.

A few minutes later he came back, towing Eddie Lowe. Reluctance was stamped on the little editor's face but he made no audible complaint. Harder shifted his tub over closer to Lowe as Verdune got ready to order them out into the water.

One by one the tubs were pushed out from the shore, the men holding them in line with their sticks anchored in the mud under the shallow water. Jim found himself almost in the middle of the line. His tub was too small to be comfortable and it was anything but a well balanced, seaworthy craft. Every move he made threatened to overturn it. His only consolation was that the others were in no better shape.

When all the tubs were in the water, Verdune fired his gun in the air as the starting signal. Poles prodded into the mud and tubs began moving slowly toward the dam.

Haste was worse than wasteful. Tom Biggs discovered that before he had covered twenty yards. He was crowding to the front, but when he tried to gain the lead with an extra strong shove on his pole, the tub suddenly flipped over

103

with the grocer underneath. A lusty shout of laughter went up from the watchers along the bank.

Jim eased up a little on his strokes. Whether he won or not mattered little to him. Getting ducked into the water did. As a result of his easy poling, he dropped behind most of the contestants. Directly ahead of him, Eddie Lowe was pushing his tub along close to the lead. His light weight was an asset in this race. Almost beside Lowe was Harder, poling furiously to keep up.

Jim didn't like the way Harder was watching Lowe. But before he realized what was in Harder's mind, the big marshal had poled his tub directly at Lowe and the two tubs bumped with a heavy jolt. Harder's tub, backed by more weight, overturned the other and Lowe splashed into the water. The crowd roared its approval, but Jim began poling ahead frantically as he saw Harder strike at Lowe with his pole. It could have been accident that he hit the editor while apparently trying to get away from the scene of the mishap, but Jim knew better.

Jim was within a few feet of the fracas when he left his tub in a long dive. The last he had seen of Lowe he was sinking, apparently unconscious. Here, closer to the dam, the water was deep enough to drown a man who couldn't swim well.

Judging his underwater progress as best he

104

could, Jim came up and hit the bottom of a tub. Grasping the edge of the tub, he heaved, and was rewarded by a yell and a splash as Harder was dumped into the pond.

Jim came to the surface then and took a look around, directing his strokes toward Lowe's over-turned tub, just sinking out of sight. Lowe came to the surface a few feet away, only half-heartedly struggling to keep afloat. With a few strong strokes, Jim came to the editor and, reaching an arm over his chest, started toward the shore only ten or twelve yards away.

Jim's feet touched bottom and he dragged Lowe to dry land. The crowd, moving along the bank, had suddenly stopped, and all attention was focused on Jim and the editor, the race forgotten.

Betty was one of the first to reach them, and her hands worked magic in helping Jim to rid Lowe's lungs of water and bring him back to full consciousness.

The race was over and the contestants were coming back along the bank to the crowd when Lowe got to his feet. Gramp pointed an accusing finger at Harder when he appeared, still dripping wet.

'You did that on purpose,' he shouted.

'That's a lie,' Harder roared. 'Nobody could guide one of those tubs. I'd like to see you try it.'

'I'll bet I could keep from running over anybody,' Gramp snapped. 'He ran into you on

105

purpose, didn't he, Eddie?'

Lowe slowly shook his head. 'Those tubs are hard to guide.'

Jim saw surprise flash over Gramp's face and felt a shock himself. But he knew what was prompting Lowe's answer. 'Eddie's got to get some dry clothes and so have I,' he said. 'Let us through.'

He guided the editor through the crowd toward Main Street. Lowe lived in the back of the building that housed the Bluestem *Bugle*, and they stopped there. Inside the office, Jim faced Lowe.

'Do you think Verdune was after you today, Eddie?'

'I know it,' Lowe said. 'He didn't like that item I put in the paper advising people to listen carefully to the speeches before making up their minds. Harder was in the office last night and gave me a lecture on that. I knew something was going to happen today when Verdune sent Noble after me to ask me to take part in the tub race.'

'That was a coward's way of striking back,' Jim said. 'Maybe you'd better watch what you print until you can get a break.'

Lowe's chin stood out in a ridged line. 'I've crawled on my belly so long now that my hide's getting thin.'

'Maybe a thin hide is better than one full of holes.'

'That's the idea Verdune was trying to get

106

across today.' Lowe suddenly dropped down on a stool. 'I suppose I'll go on crawling, but some day I'm going to get up and stand on my feet like a man.'

Jim moved to the door. 'Pick your day, Eddie, and I'll stand with you. There may come a time when we can make it worth our while.'

Jim moved down the street to his own store, certain that something more than Lowe's own conscience was crowding the editor. He couldn't blame Lowe for feeling as he did. But a dead editor would solve nobody's problems.

In dry clothes, Jim returned to the festivities. Eddie Lowe was already at the steps of the platform. Jim noticed the grin on the editor's face.

'You didn't stay out of circulation long,' Jim said.

'I couldn't. After the speeches, you know, there's a dance. And I've got a dance spoken for. Hope you don't mind.'

'Betty?'

Lowe grinned. 'That's right. But it's just one.'

'It's all right with me, Eddie. I've got no strings on her.'

Jim went up the steps to the platform, and was called on for the first speech. As he moved to the front of the platform, he read encouragement in many faces. He delivered his speech, emphasizing the reasons Verdune would have for getting rid of the herd law in the

107

western part of the state. The crowd, mostly homesteaders, cheered him lustily when he went back to his seat, and it gave him a warm feeling inside. He had done better than he had expected to.

But that warmth turned to a chill when Verdune took his turn at the speaker's stand. Ridicule was Verdune's weapon, and he used it with an art learned from years of political campaigning.

'Sending Taylor to Lincoln to represent you would be like bringing some office boy out of the city to milk your cows and plant your corn,' he said. 'Can't you just picture Taylor standing before the legislature, swaying them with his powerful oratory? Maybe he could sell them some flour and beans.'

A laugh rippled over the crowd. Verdune went on, 'If he had a good idea to present to the legislature, he wouldn't know how to put it into a bill. And he wouldn't know how to pull the ropes to get his bill acted on if he got it that far. He'd be the laughing-stock of Lincoln. You'd be better off having no representative at all.'

Verdune sat down and Jim felt the tide of sentiment swinging. The new man who had been in the surrey with Verdune this morning made the next speech. He proved to be a legislator from the eastern part of the state. He emphasized Verdune's capabilities for the office and bragged about his wonderful record

108

as a legislator when he had served before.

Jim knew it all made his speech sound pretty drab. Verdune had won the first round just as Jim had expected him to.

CHAPTER ELEVEN

Bluestem was quiet as a graveyard the day after the celebration. Jim hadn't expected anything else. While business was at a virtual standstill, he decided, would be a good time to go down to the *Bugle* office and have a talk with Eddie Lowe.

He was even with the Verdune House when he saw the horse standing in front of the printing office. He stopped. What he wanted to say to Lowe was not for publication either in the *Bugle* or by gossips. He took another look at the horse and ducked back out of sight. The horse was wearing a Flying V Bar brand.

While Jim debated if he should go back to his store to wait, two men came out of the *Bugle* office. Jim knew then that Lowe had just faced another threat, for the man mounting the horse was Bruce Noble and the dark-faced man who went across the street was Ross Harder.

Jim waited until Noble was out of town and Harder had disappeared into Biggs' store, then moved up the street to the *Bugle* office. Eddie Lowe was busy setting type, reading from a paper on the table.

109

'I see you had some company,' Jim said, going through the open door.

Lowe nodded, not looking up. 'They brought me some items to put in the next issue.'

'Well, if you're going to run a paper, you've got to have stuff to print,' Jim said carelessly.

Lowe looked up then, and there was a wild light in his eyes. 'I'm pretty busy, Jim. Couldn't you come back later?'

Jim nodded. 'It's that bad, is it? They don't want you even talking to me.'

'Harder doesn't know about me yet. But Noble has been given some hint. He made some pointed remarks. If Harder gets suspicious or if Verdune drops another hint or two—'

Jim nodded. 'Sure, Eddie, I'll leave. I just dropped by to see how you got over your ducking yesterday.'

Lowe looked out the window at Biggs' store, then went back to his work. 'Well, you've seen.'

Jim turned toward the door. A paper that had been wadded and kicked back under a desk by the door caught his eye and he picked it up. Lowe didn't look at him again, and he took the paper with him.

The courage that Eddie Lowe had shown yesterday had faded this morning in the face of the new threat Verdune had thrown at him. It probably wasn't by accident that Harder had been with Noble this morning. Jim wondered how much information Verdune had given his

110

foreman. Probably only enough to make him curious and perhaps a little suspicious. Noble was not a man to keep a secret, and Verdune wouldn't want Harder to find out about Lowe and kill him now. Verdune needed the Bluestem *Bugle*. After election, it might be a different story.

At the store, Jim smoothed out the wadded paper, and what he read brought a whistle to his lips. It was a scorching denunciation of Verdune, his tactics, and the principles for which he stood. There was an appeal to the voters to support Jim in the election. The article was not completed. Apparently Lowe's company had come on the scene before he finished, and he had wadded the paper and stuffed it under his desk.

For Lowe's own good, it was lucky Noble and Harder had visited him this morning.

Betty came to town that afternoon. Her enthusiasm was at a high pitch when she hurried into the store. She handed Jim a list of groceries and a couple of items Gramp had sent for.

'Fill this while I talk,' she said. 'Things are looking good for us now.'

Jim shook his head. 'I don't see it. Not after the speech I made yesterday.'

'I was talking to Mr. Ostrand after the speeches. He told me some things you should put into your future talks. Besides, if we can get the press on our side, we can swing a lot of votes our way.'

'Don't count on the press, Betty. Verdune has everything in this town sewed up tight.'

Betty smiled knowingly. 'Not everything, Jim. You're going to be elected, and the Bluestem *Bugle* will do it.'

'Being elected to the legislature isn't so important as being able to do something for the homesteaders when I get there.'

'You'll do a lot for the settlers once you're elected. And I'm going to have a finger in helping elect you. We'll be somebody important then. More important than Claude Verdune or that snippy daughter of his.'

Jim saw the light in her eyes and knew what she was thinking. The wife of a legislator would automatically be the society queen of any community. A moment of doubt swept over him. Was it Jim Taylor she wanted to marry, or was it a seat in the legislature?

'Don't be disappointed at anything you read in the *Bugle*, Betty. Remember, Eddie Lowe is Verdune's man. He may not like it, but he is, and he can't do anything about it.'

'He can do something,' Betty said spiritedly. 'And he will. Any man can do what he pleases if he's strong enough.'

'He can until he runs into someone stronger. Eddie Lowe is a fine chap, but he isn't the strongest man in the world.'

Betty frowned. 'Eddie promised me yesterday that he'd support you in this

112

campaign. Are you trying to tell me he's backing out?'

'You don't understand Verdune and the way he fights. He's got gunmen with itchy fingers around him. I don't think Lowe is a fool. He would be if he switched to our side now. And he'd be a dead fool within a week.'

Betty turned to the window and stood looking silently out into the street. Finally she faced Jim again. 'Do you think Verdune would go that far?'

'I'll bet my store he would. I figure he'll do anything to keep from being licked. He knows he has to have the *Bugle* backing him. He'll make sure it stays under his control.'

'But Eddie promised.'

'Don't hold him to it, Betty. Unless you want him dead.'

'All right, Jim,' she said after a moment. 'We'll wait. But we'll find a way to stop those editorials.'

'Something may break. If it does, Eddie can do us more good then than he can now.'

'Maybe you're right. Mr. Ostrand says we should challenge Verdune to a debate in October. By then all the issues will be clear and you'll have the side of the argument that will appeal to the homesteaders.'

'I can't debate against Verdune.'

'You can't beat him by hiding. By October you'll know how to handle him. We'll win this fall. You'll see.'

She went out, wheeled her horse and went back up the street.

*   *   *

July and August slipped away, with the campaign smoldering along, threatening to flare up when the weather cooled. Jim was dreading it. Nothing had broken in his favor. The *Bugle* had stayed under Verdune's wing and blasted Jim repeatedly. Ward's homesteaders were remaining staunchly behind Jim, but he couldn't be sure whether the homesteaders downstream were listening to the arguments he and Gramp were putting up or reading and believing what the *Bugle* printed.

The days were getting shorter and the lights were blazing earlier than usual when Jim escorted Betty into the hall for a Saturday night dance late in September. The Flying V Bar was there, as were most of the homesteaders from both above and below town. The same tenseness was in the air that had been there at every dance for the last month. And each week it seemed to grow tighter.

As the music began, Jim and Betty moved out on the floor. Betty, still confident of victory with election only five weeks away, had instilled some of her enthusiasm in Jim but not much of her confidence.

Stormy was here with Chester Fyfe as she

had been every Saturday night. Rumor had it that their wedding day was not far off. In spite of that rumor, Jim always claimed his dance with Stormy. Fyfe showed his displeasure but never interfered.

Tonight Jim watched for his chance after a young homesteader from down the creek had taken Betty from him. When the music stopped he was among the first to reach Stormy. She shrugged off one of the Flying V Bar punchers, sending him scowling to the stag line, and turned to Jim.

'How much longer is your dad going to allow you to be seen with me?' Jim asked, noticing the eyes of the crowd on them.

'He allows lots of things he doesn't like,' she said easily as the music started and they fell in step. 'He never comes to these dances and he couldn't do anything about it if he were here.'

Jim had the feeling that Stormy's desire to prove to the world that she was her own boss was the chief reason she held this weekly dance open for him.

'I hear you're thinking of accepting a new boss,' Jim said, nodding toward Fyfe.

'I've heard that, too.'

He waited for her to elaborate but she said no more. He realized he had been put in his place.

'Are you ready for the debate?' Stormy asked, switching the subject to point at him.

'I'll be ready when the time comes,' he said

115

with more confidence than he felt.

She laughed. 'You know you'll never be ready to debate against dad. You should have learned that on the Fourth of July.'

'I've learned several things since then,' he said quickly, feeling the barb of her words.

'Maybe you'll make the debate interesting enough to attract a crowd,' she said. 'That's what we're hoping. I suppose you've got other things than the election on your mind.'

He frowned, trying to follow her thought. 'Meaning?'

She nodded toward the door. 'Your sodbuster friend and Eddie Lowe. They just went out the door. Think it's only business?'

Irritation and uncertainty brought the color into his face. 'Why not?'

'Want to bet?'

'Name the stakes.'

'A box of chocolate candy.'

Jim nodded. 'It's a bet. Now how are you going to prove I'm wrong?'

'Let's go see.' She took his arm and led him toward the door. Jim glanced around and saw Fyfe scowling after them. That alone, he decided, was worth a box of candy. And how could he lose? He was certain that Betty, in spite of the warning he had given her, was trying to persuade Eddie Lowe to switch sides.

The air was cool, almost chilly, but Jim gave it little thought as he followed Stormy out toward the long hitchrack that ran the length of the hall. Suddenly Stormy caught his arm and drew him back into the shadows.

'See,' she whispered, pointing to a rig halfway down the line.

Jim looked, recognizing the team and rig as one from the livery barn. Lowe was helping Betty into the buggy.

Jim started to back around the corner of the building, but Stormy checked him. 'Stick around, Jim. I want to win that bet.'

'What's wrong with her taking a ride with him?' he asked lamely, knowing exactly what was wrong in the eyes of Bluestem society when one man's girl went riding with another man.

'No more wrong with that than with one man's girl saving a dance for another man every Saturday night,' she said pointedly. 'But right there the similarity ends. Just keep watching.'

Jim kept watching, although he wished he were somewhere else.

He saw Lowe go around the buggy and climb into the seat beside Betty. But they didn't back away from the hitchrack. Although they were talking earnestly, their words didn't span the gap between the buggy and Jim.

Then a wave of despair rolled over Jim. The shadows were deep under the buggy top, but not deep enough to conceal the fact that Betty had snuggled close in the editor's arms. Jim turned back toward the hall and met Stormy's eyes. But there was no triumph in her face.

'Funny business, isn't it?' she said softly, and

followed him back to the front door.

Fyfe met them at the door, and anger was bright in his face. But Jim brushed him off as if he were a bothersome fly. He didn't remember exactly how he spent the rest of the evening. A dozen questions plagued him. But there were no answers to any of them.

Betty and Eddie weren't gone long. And when they came back into the hall, Betty was her usual self. Jim kept his feelings to himself, but as he took her home, he brought the editor into the conversation.

'He'll be on our side before election,' Betty said confidently. 'I took a buggy ride with him tonight, and he's almost ready to strike back at Verdune.'

Jim held back what was uppermost in his mind. 'You know what that will mean. His life won't be worth one of his weekly editions.'

'He has considered that. I don't think it's that bad, Jim. He's willing to take any chances necessary.'

'Are you? You wouldn't want him dead, would you?'

She looked up, shock in her face. 'Of course not, Jim. I—'

'No use pretending, Betty,' he said. 'I happened to be outside tonight when you started for that ride.'

'Oh.' She dropped her eyes and said no more until they were almost to the homesteads. 'I didn't mean to let that happen, Jim,' she said

118

then.

'Forget it,' he said.

'I can't, Jim. I don't want you to think I deliberately doublecrossed you.'

'Eddie's quite a fellow, isn't he?'

She nodded. 'You'll never know how fine until you really get acquainted with him.'

'I can guess.'

'This won't change a thing so far as the campaign is concerned except Eddie will boost you every chance he gets.'

'Tell him to be careful how he boosts. I don't want him dead, either.'

Gramp came into the store a few days later, and excitement was bubbling through his words.

'I'm on the track of something, Jim, that will slide you right into Lincoln.'

Jim grinned. His enthusiasm for the legislative job had hit a new low, and Gramp's excitement seemed foolish. 'Somebody going to shoot Verdune?'

Gramp looked over the store, frowning when he saw Ross Harder in the far end, apparently engrossed in an examination of some guns Jim had on display. 'What I've got to say ain't for nobody's ears but yours.'

'Put on the muffler and nobody will hear you,' Jim said softly.

'I'll wait,' Gramp said. 'But I'll tell you this much. What I'm on the track of now will really tie a knot in Verdune's tail. I'll have it here by

119

the time you take on Verdune in that debate.'

'Something about his past record?' Jim asked, realizing that Gramp was in earnest.

'It's a past record, all right,' Gramp said. 'But I ain't telling who or what. Donkeys have long ears, you know.'

Gramp spun on his heel, and Jim turned his eyes on Harder. There was a scowl on the marshal's face, and Jim knew that he had heard at least part of what they had said. Harder left the store and Jim watched Gramp ride out of town. At the end of the street Gramp met another rider coming into town. Jim grinned a little as he turned to the counter by his cash drawer. From under the counter he brought out a small box. With it, he went out to the hitchrack. The rider, seeing him, turned in.

'I pay my debts,' Jim said, holding the box out to Stormy. 'One box of chocolates was the bet, I believe.'

She laughed. 'Right. But maybe I'll just call it a present. It might remind somebody that girls like to be given presents. Thanks, Jim.'

She rode on down the street, and Jim turned back into the store.

CHAPTER TWELVE

Jim Taylor had known some days of unrest and indecision but nothing to compare with this. Since morning he had tried to get his speech in

120

readiness for tomorrow's debate with Verdune. He would have the stand first and he wanted to make a good impression. It would be his last chance, he knew. Verdune would hog the show from then on.

He saw Harder leave town that afternoon and he wondered what could be taking the marshal away from his duty. Something at the Flying V Bar, Jim would bet on that. But he soon forgot Harder as Gramp worked back into his mind. The old fellow had been in the store this morning on his way to McCook, and he had been as excited as a child. He wouldn't say much, but there had been a mysterious twinkle in his eyes. Jim decided he was going after that magic something that was to put the skids under Verdune.

A half-dozen homesteaders dropped in to make purchases and to tell him they were pulling for him in the debate tomorrow. That constant reminder of the faith and trust the settlers were putting in him added weight to his determination to give Verdune the best battle he could.

It was late afternoon when a rider galloped into town and pulled up at Jim's hitchrack. Jim didn't know the man and there was no brand on the horse. A new homesteader, Jim guessed. The man, a short, squat fellow, came into the store.

'Got a message for Jim Taylor,' he said.

'I'm Taylor.' Jim came around the counter.

121

'Who's it from?'

'An old fellow named Shepherd.'

A premonition of disaster swept over Jim. But he shook it off. 'Gramp went to McCook,' he said.

'Maybe he changed his mind.' The man held out a folded paper. 'He paid me to deliver this to you.'

Jim took the paper, and the messenger turned and hurried out of the store. Jim unfolded the paper. He had never seen Gramp's handwriting, but the almost illegible scrawl could easily be his, he decided. He read it quickly.

'I got what I wanted without going to McCook. Come out as soon as you can. I've got news for you.'

It was signed 'Gramp.' Jim read it a second and third time. Nothing seemed wrong. But Jim couldn't understand why the old fellow hadn't come to town with his news. He read the note again and his doubts persisted. But regardless of his doubts, he had to investigate.

He closed the store earlier than usual and went to the livery barn for his horse. Before sundown he was on his way up the river trail toward Gramp's homestead.

Dusk had settled over the prairie before he reached the fork in the trail that turned away from the creek toward the homesteads. A covey of quail broke out of the tall grass along the creek and whirled away with startling

122

speed. Jim relaxed, and a peace crept into him such as he hadn't known for a month. He watched a dozen mallards coast down toward a wide pool in the creek, think better of landing so close to him, and rise again with a staccato chorus of quacks.

He left the creek and soon was within sight of Gramp's buildings. Here he reined down to a walk. Everything was quiet around the place. It wasn't like Gramp to hole up in the house until it was pitch dark.

A hundred yards from the house, Jim stopped. The chug of a prairie chicken came from off to his right, but there was no sound ahead. Nothing about the place seemed amiss. It was just too quiet. The dusk deepened and the shadows folded in around the buildings as Jim waited.

Then suddenly a light sprang up in the window of the soddy. Jim grinned in relief and nudged his horse ahead. Gramp must be lighting his kerosene lamp.

He reached the hitchrack and swung down, then turned to go inside. It was there he stopped, a chill running down his back. Ross Harder was standing just across the hitchrack from him, and Chester Fyfe was back in the doorway.

'Coming to see Gramp?' Harder asked easily.

'I didn't come to see you,' Jim said sharply. 'Where's Gramp?'

'I heard him tell you this morning he was going to McCook. Doesn't he usually do what he says?'

Jim knew he had been tricked. 'What's on your mind, Harder?' he asked, inching back to put a little daylight between him and the marshal and to free his gun hand, which was crowded against his horse.

'We just came over to pay Shepherd a visit. Since he's gone, we'll have to settle for a visit with you.'

The stalling irritated Jim almost as much as the fact that he had so conveniently played into their hands. Harder was like a big cat playing with his mouse before he killed it.

'I'm not in a visiting mood, Harder,' Jim said. 'If Gramp's gone, I'll head back to town.'

Harder came around the hitchrack, and Jim considered throwing his gun. He knew Harder's reputation for gunspeed, but Jim felt his equal now. Over in the doorway, however, Fyfe had slipped his hand inside his coat, and Jim didn't miss the significance of that. If he drew on Harder, Fyfe would cut him down. Jim waited, mentally weighing a new idea that had just struck him. He didn't tab Fyfe as one who would tangle in a rough and tumble brawl, and if Harder got close enough—

'Just to make sure you stay friendly,' Harder said as he came closer to Jim, 'I'd better take your gun. Unbuckle your belt.'

Jim didn't move. 'If you want it, Harder,

124

come and get it.'

Harder stopped, and Jim saw the expression on his face change. A sneer twisted his features; then it disappeared and a serious frown took its place. Evidently he hadn't expected this kind of trouble with Fyfe backing his play.

For an instant Jim thought the marshal was going to step forward to take the gun. But he jerked at his own weapon instead. Jim struck with the swiftness of a hawk. One hand caught Harder's wrist as he lunged forward, and the other lashed a cutting blow into the marshal's face.

Harder reeled back, but Jim didn't let him go. Out of the corner of his eye, he saw that Fyfe had drawn a small gun and was holding it ready to use if he got the chance. Jim crowded close to Harder as he staggered backward.

The marshal was a strong man and he rallied quickly, forgetting the gun and striking out with his fists. The joyous light of battle was in his eyes, but Jim quickly dimmed that light. He countered Harder's sweeping uppercut with a solid jolt straight to the marshal's unprotected nose, a nose Jim had broken last spring. Blood spurted and Harder howled as he backed away. But Jim was right on him, never letting him break free.

Fyfe came out of the doorway, waving his gun excitedly, calling for Harder to push Jim away so he could use the gun. But Jim gave

Fyfe no target, pummeling Harder with short jabs while hanging on to the big man. Suddenly a bullet ripped into the dirt at the fighters' feet, just nicking Jim's leg as it passed.

'Don't shoot, you idiot!' Harder screamed. 'Hit him.'

Jim caught the marshal's arm and whirled him toward Fyfe, then jabbed his fist deep into the pit of his stomach. Breath exploded out of the big man and he doubled up as he rocked back on his heels. But Fyfe was too quick to be caught. He sidestepped and swung his gun around toward Jim. Jim lunged forward, landing on Harder and rolling with him on the ground.

Jim was at a disadvantage in a rough and tumble fight with the big marshal, even though Harder was out of breath from the blow Jim had landed. As Harder's strength came back, the tide of the battle quickly swung his way. He got his arms around Jim and began squeezing, thumping him in the ribs with his fists.

Jim knew he had to break that grip. Drawing his knees up for a pry, he straightened suddenly. Harder's grip broke and he rolled one way, Jim the other. As he came to his feet Jim saw Fyfe bearing down on him, swinging half of a broken neck-yoke. But he couldn't avoid the blow. His last thought was that he was failing Gramp and the homesteaders . . . .

It seemed to Jim he had never known such inky blackness as that which engulfed him when his mind began working again. His first thought was that the blow on his head had left him blind. His head ached furiously. He lay still and tried to remember what had happened before the blow.

Gradually it all returned to him, the message from Gramp and then the fight. He sat up, holding his head against the throbbing ache that threatened to split his skull. As his brain slowly cleared, he realized that his hands and feet were not tied. Then another of his sense registered a report. The air had a dank smell. Only one place could smell like that. A cellar. He was in Gramp's cellar. The cave behind his store had this same odor, cool and wet and musty.

Reaching out a hand, he touched the wall. A thin coating of plaster had been put over the dirt to keep it from caving in. He got to his feet and felt his way along the wall. Gramp had dug steps out of the dirt, and Jim tried to find them now.

'Jim.' The voice came out of the darkness beside him, and it was barely above a whisper. He whirled, his hand instinctively slapping his thigh for a gun that wasn't there.

For an instant he stood facing the voice, trying to collect his startled wits. It was a girl's voice, and in another second he realized it belonged to Stormy Verdune. But here in Gramp's cellar was the last place in Verdune County he would have expected to find her.

'What are you doing here?' Jim demanded, fumbling in his pocket for a match.

He struck the match, and the light flickered over the little cellar, revealing Stormy leaning against the wall. There was none of the pride and independence in her face that he had always associated with her. She was frightened, and in her eyes was the look of a trapped animal.

'They carried you halfway down the steps and threw you in,' she said as if she hadn't heard his question. 'Then they shut the door and put a heavy weight on it. I can't budge it.'

'I've already figured out how I got here,' Jim said. 'But I doubt if you got here the same way.'

Her eyes lowered just before the match burned down to Jim's fingers and he had to drop it. 'I came to see what was going to happen, and I hid here in the cellar so Ross Harder and Chester wouldn't see me.'

'How could you help them that way?' Jim asked sarcastically.

'This was Chester's idea,' she admitted. 'Dad didn't approve.'

'Chester's quite a man.' Jim clamped his teeth against the words that boiled up inside him. This was no time for arguing, not even with Stormy. There must be some way to get out of the cellar.

He felt his way to the steps he had seen in the flicker of the match's light. He went up until his head and shoulders hit the door. Then he lifted until it seemed his head would burst with the effort. But the door didn't give. They had it weighted down so an ox team wouldn't move it. He turned back into the cellar.

'There's an old basket here,' Stormy said. 'And there's a little vent hole straight above us. Maybe we could burn this basket for light.'

'A lot of good light will do us,' Jim said. But he got another match and nursed a sliver of the basket into a tiny blaze.

'I'm sorry you're in this, Jim,' Stormy said as the blaze lit up the interior of the little cellar.

'Why should you be?' he demanded, still smarting from the memory of the ease with which Fyfe had trapped him. 'This will set things up fine for your dad. He'll have the platform all to himself tomorrow. And he'll make hay out of the fact that I don't show up.'

'I told you he'd make a monkey of you, Jim,' Stormy said, but there was no triumph in her voice. 'He knows, like everyone else, that you've been worried about this debate. He'll say you were afraid to meet him and ran out. Whatever reason you give when you go back, he'll call it an excuse.'

Jim strode angrily around the tiny cellar. 'Well, he'll be elected without opposition now.'

Stormy frowned, some color coming back into her cheeks. 'He would be, anyway. This won't make any difference in the outcome of the election.'

'Then why did they lock me in here?'

129

Jim startled himself with the question. He hadn't pictured himself as a really serious threat to Claude Verdune in the election. But Fyfe surely must have.

'Maybe I was partly to blame,' Stormy admitted. 'I kept telling them you wouldn't be so easy to beat as they thought. Chester is not one to take chances. He wanted to be sure.'

'He should be sure now,' Jim said in disgust.

'I had nothing to do with this scheme,' Stormy said earnestly. 'If I had, do you think I'd be locked in here, too?'

He hadn't considered that. He shrugged. 'I'm not blaming you. But that doesn't get us out.'

'I've had longer to think about our predicament than you have. The dirt here is sandy. Can't we dig out?'

Jim looked over the cellar quickly. The roof was too high to reach, and it was made of heavy timber covered with dirt. They couldn't escape that way. But the walls were different. Only the coating of plaster covered the sandy ground.

'Anything sharp in here?' Jim asked, the listlessness of defeat gone from his voice.

'Nothing except these jars of canned fruit,' Stormy said, pointing to a row of glass jars along the far end of the cellar.

Betty had canned that fruit for Gramp, Jim thought, but she wouldn't object to wasting one jar to help him escape and strike back at Verdune.

130

'We'll break a jar,' Jim said. 'If I can get a hole in this plaster, I can use the glass to dig through the dirt.'

Stormy broke the jar and handed a big piece of glass to Jim. He stood back and kicked at the plaster. It was thicker than he had thought, but it finally cracked and a big chunk fell out. Jim tore away more of it until he had a hole three feet square. Then he began digging at the dirt.

He had expected the sandy loam to be soft, but it wasn't. He realized it was going to take a lot of work to tunnel out enough dirt for Stormy and him to escape. But he had no choice. There was no other way of getting out of the cellar except to wait until Gramp came home or Fyfe and Harder came back to release him. That wouldn't be until after the debate. And that would be too late.

Jim dug until his hand was cramped from holding the broken glass. When he stopped to rest, Stormy took the glass from him, crawled into the little hole he had started and took her turn at the work.

'If you help too much, I may get out in time to make that debate,' Jim said. 'Your dad won't like that.'

'That's his worry,' Stormy said spiritedly. 'I want to get out of here.'

Jim grinned and after letting Stormy dig for a few minutes, went back to work. The night wore on. Jim's watch had been broken in the fight and he had no way of knowing what time

131

it was. He was nearly exhausted when he broke into softer dirt and realized he was nearly to the surface where a rain last week had softened the ground.

Five minutes later, he pushed the dirt back from the rim of the hole he had bored and pulled himself up into the morning sunlight. Reaching down, he helped Stormy out. They pounded the dust out of their clothes and Stormy drew a deep breath.

'I never thought sunlight would look so good.'

Jim looked at Gramp's soddy. 'That house looks good to me. Gramp ought to have something to eat there.'

They crossed to the house and went inside; Stormy motioned to the bed against the far wall. 'You rest,' she said. 'I'll get some breakfast. I'm starved.'

Jim was too tired to argue. He was asleep when Stormy shook him and announced that breakfast was ready. She seemed in good spirits in spite of the hectic night. As Jim's hunger began to fade, worry about the speech he was going to make at the debate began twisting his thoughts.

A light spring wagon wheeled into the yard and Jim hurried to the door, wishing he had a gun. But he grinned in relief as he saw Gramp wrap the lines around the whipstock and hop out.

'What's been going on here?' Gramp

demanded before he reached the house. 'By Henry, it looks like a tornado tangled with a passel of badgers.' He pointed through the door at Stormy. 'What's she doing here?'

Jim told him quickly and asked about his trip to McCook.

Gramp shook his head sadly. 'Not a thing yet, Jim. But it's coming. I ain't going to tell you what it is till it gets here, so you won't be too disappointed if it doesn't show up in time.'

'I didn't expect you back until tonight,' Jim said.

'I drove mighty nigh all night so I could get back in time for the debate. My team's played out. Now you tell them today what happened to you, Jim. I'll back you up, and if anybody doubts us, I'll invite them out to see what my place looks like. They even took the wheels off my heavy lumber wagon to put on the cellar door. And that hole you dug would accommodate a bear.' Gramp frowned at Stormy. 'What about you?'

'I'm going home,' Stormy said. 'I don't want to hear about last night again. But, Jim, I do wish you luck.'

Bluestem was buzzing when Jim and Gramp got to town. A shout went up from the homesteaders when they spotted Jim. Verdune was in town, too, and Jim learned before he dismounted that the word had already been spread far and wide that he had run out rather than face Verdune in a debate which he had no chance of winning.

Jim got his horse put away just in time for the debate to begin. He saw Fyfe and Harder conferring with Verdune, and there were worried frowns on their faces. Jim's escape evidently had upset their plans.

Jim mounted the steps to the porch of Biggs' store where the debate was to be held, and the noise of the crowd subsided to a murmur.

'Hey, where have you been?' some man in the back of the crowd yelled. 'We don't like people who are late.'

Jim didn't have to be told that the heckler was a Verdune man. 'If you'll look at your watch,' he said, 'you'll find that I'm not late. I've told you before why I'm running for the legislature. This is farmer country now. This district needs a legislator who will represent the farmer as well as the rancher. The herd law is fair to both. No man, whether he be rancher or farmer, should want his stock to range farther than the boundaries of his own land. My opponent says he will not try to change the herd law if he is elected, even though it would be to his advantage to do so. I challenge him to sign a written oath to that effect. Unless he does take such an oath, you can be certain that he intends to abolish that law. And that will mean the end of farming in any territory where he can range his cattle.'

An approving murmur went up. While Jim waited for the noise to subside, he wondered if

134

he had made a good move. If Verdune signed such a pledge, regardless of his intentions to keep it, he would get plenty of support from the homesteaders. But if he wouldn't sign such an oath, the farmer vote that Verdune had planned on getting would melt away.

Verdune's face told nothing of what was going on in his mind. But Harder's scowl was there for all to see, and Fyfe was having a difficult time keeping his feelings hidden. It was obvious they didn't like this turn of affairs.

Jim kept the rest of his speech short. Then he stepped down and let Verdune take over. The applause for the big rancher was weak, coming entirely from the town's merchants and the Flying V Bar riders who were present. And Verdune's speech lacked the vigor he had shown in his Fourth of July address. He made no mention of Jim's challenge and Jim knew that, for the first time, he had not come off second best to Verdune.

Before Verdune had finished his talk, Gramp moved around to Jim and tugged at his elbow. 'You ninny,' he whispered, 'why don't you tell what happened to you last night? That's all it will take now to finish Verdune.'

'We'd better let well enough alone,' Jim advised. 'We'll use that if we have to.'

But Gramp was not one to let any advantage get away. When Verdune came down from the porch at the end of his speech, Gramp leaped up in his place.

135

'Hold on a minute, gents,' Gramp yelled in his shrill voice. 'There's something else you ought to know. Jim was out of town this morning for a reason. Verdune sent his town marshal, Harder, and his right hand man, Fyfe, to my place last night, after having a fake message delivered to Jim to get him out there. Those two brave boys jumped Jim and knocked him out and put him in my cellar. They piled the wheels off my lumber wagon against the door so he couldn't get out. They were afraid of him. Jim had to dig his way out.'

'There's not a word of truth in that,' Verdune interrupted from the steps of the porch. 'I gave no such orders. Can't you see that Shepherd knows that Taylor can't win by fair tactics, so he's trying to blacken my reputation?'

'If you don't believe every word I'm saying,' Gramp shouted to the crowd, 'come out to my place and I'll show you.'

A rider had raced into town while the crowd listened to Gramp. Jim watched him go directly to Fyfe and Harder, and in a moment Verdune had been brought into the circle of their conference. Then, while the crowd was still buzzing about Gramp's revelations, Verdune leaped back up on the porch beside Gramp, waving his hand for silence.

'What Shepherd has just been telling you is a cooked-up scheme to discredit me,' Verdune declared angrily when the noise subsided. 'Now

136

I want to tell you something that will open your eyes. My daughter, Stormy, has been missing since yesterday afternoon. She just got back to the ranch a short time ago. One of my men rode in to tell me. She was kidnapped and held captive all night by none other than my opponent, Jim Taylor.'

A roar of surprise greeted the words. Jim was stunned. He looked at Fyfe and saw the smug grin of satisfaction on his face. Verdune waved his hand for silence again. The anger was gone from his face now, and once more he was a master politician driving home a point.

'Taylor threatened to hold my daughter captive indefinitely if I didn't withdraw from the legislative race. But she escaped this morning.'

'Where was he holding her?' a doubting voice yelled.

The question seemed to please Verdune. 'At Gramp Shepherd's homestead. If you'll go out there, you'll probably find, as Shepherd says, all those wagon wheels on the cellar door and a big hole dug into the cellar. Taylor and Shepherd did that last night so they could back up this crazy story they told this morning.'

It was a good story Fyfe had cooked up on such short notice. There were several spots that were hardly logical, but the people listening to Verdune were too excited by the sensational tale to test it for weaknesses. But one homesteader, not so easily convinced, voiced a

137

protest.

'Gramp went to McCook yesterday.'

Verdune and Fyfe exchanged quick glances; then Verdune turned back to the crowd. 'That's where he said he was going. But he's right here this morning, you'll notice. Do you know of anybody who ordinarily drives a spring wagon from here to McCook and back in one day?'

That put the clincher on Verdune's argument. Jim looked at Gramp, expecting a loud angry denial, but for once the old fellow seemed to be speechless. Verdune had won the day.

CHAPTER THIRTEEN

It was the next day before Jim realized the lengths to which Verdune and Fyfe would go to swing votes to the big rancher. He heard it first when he stopped in at the office of the *Bugle* to see what Lowe was going to print about the debate.

'I'm not going to print everything they're saying,' Lowe said angrily. 'I know it's not so. They can take a whack at you and call it politics. But when they start dragging in women and smearing their characters, that's too much.'

Jim frowned. 'Who are they dragging in? Betty?'

Lowe shook his head. 'It's someone you wouldn't expect. It's Stormy. They're making mighty broad hints about you and her and the time you had her kidnapped.'

Jim swallowed his amazement. 'That will fix me politically, all right. But think what it will do to Stormy.'

'It won't help your standing as a man, either. And there are always plenty of people ready to believe anything bad about someone else. Some people seem to live for no other purpose than to spread tales like that.'

Jim turned toward the door. 'What are you going to print, Eddie?'

'As little as possible. And nothing on that story about you and Stormy.'

Jim went back to his store. He felt sick. He could stand Verdune's cries about his incompetence, even the story he started yesterday about his being afraid to debate with him, but this last blow cut deep and brought out an anger he hadn't known since the campaign started.

Betty rode into town before the sun was halfway to the zenith. She came straight to the store, and Jim didn't have to ask if she had heard the stories making the rounds.

'What are you going to do about it?' she demanded.

'Nothing right now,' he said. 'All I could do is deny it, and they'd twist anything I say into an admission of guilt. Verdune has his cards played just right.'

'Verdune! Verdune!' Betty snapped, whirling

toward the window. 'That's all I hear. Isn't there any way of beating him?'

'I don't know,' Jim said. 'I thought we had him on the run yesterday, but you know how he twisted around that story Gramp told.'

'Aren't you going to fight?'

Jim's lips tightened. 'I'll fight if I can find a way. But it shouldn't matter so much to you now if I do lose the election.'

She turned from the window and looked straight at him. 'I'm still in this fight, Jim. I'm a homesteader. And the homesteaders aren't backing down from Verdune. I want you to be elected just as much as I ever did—even if it may be for a different reason.'

'I'm glad to hear that, Betty,' Jim said earnestly. 'But what can I do that won't play right into Verdune's hands?'

'You can't just sit here, Jim. You've got to do something.'

'I'm not the only one involved in this now, remember.'

Betty nodded slowly. 'I know. For the first time, I feel sorry for Stormy Verdune. I wonder how she feels, having her own family turn against her.'

'Verdune is using Stormy as a pawn to gain his own ends,' Jim said. 'Anything that gets in his way or can be used to his advantage will be treated the same.'

A rider came into the far end of the street and raced toward the center of town, jerking up in front of the Verdune House. Jim and Betty were at the window watching as Stormy Verdune hit the dirt and ran up the steps to the veranda of the hotel.

'She's really mad,' Betty said softly. 'And I don't blame her.'

'What's she doing in town?' Jim asked, bewildered. 'Seems like this would be the last place she would want to come.'

'Probably is,' Betty said. 'But where else could she go? And if she has any spunk she won't stay with Verdune now.'

Jim nodded. 'She's got spunk, all right.'

'I think I'll go see her.' Betty moved toward the door.

'You two don't get along,' Jim reminded her.

'We will now,' Betty said wisely, and went out into the street.

She was back in less than ten minutes, and the excitement in her face told Jim that she had not made her call in vain.

'She's ready to kill Verdune,' Betty announced. 'I think things are going to pop now. I'm going down to see Eddie.'

'Don't crowd Eddie too far, Betty,' Jim warned. 'We might be without an editor some morning if you do.'

'I'll be careful how much I say. I told Stormy you'd be over this afternoon to see her.'

Jim could guess what Betty had in mind, but he asked, frowning, 'Why?'

'Because she asked for you. You go over

141

there and talk to her. If you don't see why you're there after listening to her for five minutes, you're too slow-witted to be in the legislature, anyway.'

'She won't help me against her own stepfather,' Jim said, wondering as he said it if his argument wasn't just a brake against his own optimism.

'She's mad, Jim. Madder than you've ever seen a woman.'

'She'll get over it.'

Betty shook her head. 'You've got some things to learn. One is that a woman's wrath is more dangerous than a gunman on the rampage.'

Betty stayed in town until afternoon, and Jim guessed she was waiting to see how he made out with Stormy. He went to the Verdune House after dinner, got a knowing leer from the clerk when he asked for Stormy's room, and went up to the second floor.

'I was looking for you,' she said when she opened the door to his knock.

He hesitated, remembering what a gossip the clerk downstairs was. 'Maybe I shouldn't have come.'

'Let them talk. They're talking, anyway.' Stormy's black eyes were flashing.

'I'm sorry about this,' Jim said, wishing he knew just what to say.

'So am I,' Stormy said bitterly. 'But it's not your fault. I don't know whether it was

142

Claude's idea or Chester's to start these stories.' She clenched her fists. 'They're both going to pay.'

Jim noticed that she didn't call Verdune Dad, and he remembered that Betty had said she was mad enough to kill Verdune. 'What are you aiming to do?' he asked, watching her closely.

'That's up to you. Do you want me to help you win an election?'

'How?'

Her eyes sparkled in anticipation. 'By using the same tactics on Claude that he's been using on you. Only I'll tell the truth. I couldn't think of anything more rotten than the truth.'

'Verdune will twist it around so it will look like he's lily white. Look how he squirmed out of the spot we put him in yesterday.'

'He won't wiggle out of the stories I'll tell. And people will believe me, too.'

Jim crossed to the window of the room. 'What makes you think they'll believe you if Verdune denies what you say?'

'I'll furnish proof,' Stormy said forcibly. 'And I'll prove so many things they can't overlook them all.'

Jim hesitated. He wondered how long that anger would burn against the man she had called Dad for so many years. 'You'll change your mind, Stormy. After all, Claude Verdune has been a father to you.'

Stormy wheeled on him, and Jim felt the lash

143

of her temper. 'He hasn't been a father to me. Would any father treat his daughter like he's treated me? I've tried to be a daughter to him, even though I've never really liked him. I've helped him all I could in this campaign. You see the reward I get for it. Now it's his turn. It will nearly kill him to get beaten in this election. It will ruin his pride and break his grip on this end of the county. I'm going to enjoy every minute of it.'

Jim marveled at her fury. Right now, at least, there could be no question about her sincerity.

'Doesn't he have clear title to most of his land?' Jim asked, wondering how much Stormy really knew about Verdune's dealings.

'Only a little,' Stormy said. 'He's laying claim to thousands of acres he has no right to. Some of it he got in crooked deals. Some of it he is holding by bluff. An investigation would show that he got this quarter that Bluestem sits on in a swindle. He fully expects to own the entire western half of Verdune County before he is through. His first big step is to get elected to the legislature. He knows how to twist the laws and the lawmakers down in Lincoln so he can get what he wants. I aim to stop him if I can, and I want him to know that I was the one who did it.'

Jim thought of her offer to help him and knew he had no choice. Maybe she would relent in her stand against Verdune. But what could he lose? Without her help, he didn't have a ghost of a show against Verdune.

'I'm ready to team up with you, Stormy,' he said. 'You hold the high cards. So you deal them and I'll play them. What ideas do you have?'

'I don't have any ideas yet,' Stormy said, walking to the window. 'But I have the facts and I'll think of ways to use them.'

A knock on the door brought Stormy around, a wild light springing into her eyes. She darted to an open satchel on the bed and picked up a small revolver. Then she faced the door. Jim, his own gun in his hand, stepped back to the corner as she called for the visitor to come in.

The door opened. Jim relaxed and Stormy sighed in relief as Eddie Lowe rushed in, followed by Betty.

'Betty tells me you're siding with Jim,' Lowe said.

'That's right,' Stormy said. 'And I don't care who knows it.'

'This is the break I've been waiting for.' Lowe turned bright eyes toward Jim. 'I'm going to blow the lid off this thing with my next issue. I'll tell the voters something that will wake them up.'

Jim knew there was no stopping Eddie Lowe now. Stormy's revolt was the match that had lit the fuse. But it was Stormy herself who put the brakes on the editor's enthusiasm.

'Take it easy, Eddie,' she said thoughtfully. 'I

145

think I'm getting my teeth into something now. You're planning to tell the whole world about yourself and how you happen to be Claude Verdune's slave. Right?'

'Exactly,' Lowe said. 'This will wake up people. I'll get into trouble, but I can't stand this boot licking any longer.'

Stormy shook her head. 'If you do that, you'll have just one choice. You'll either die like a man or die like a coward. If you knew Claude Verdune as well as I do, you wouldn't print that story and expect to live.'

'Stormy's right,' Jim agreed.

Lowe frowned and paced the floor. 'Do you want me to go on printing all those lies he gives me? We can't lick him that way.'

'I said I had an idea,' Stormy reminded him. 'We'll steal a page right out of his own book on political maneuvers. I've got some things to tell about him that will make your yarn sound tame. We'll make up a special edition of the paper and put all these stories in it. Then we'll hold it until the day before election. That won't give him time to fight back.'

Jim whistled softly. It was a sound piece of strategy Stormy had proposed.

But he saw one obstacle. 'How are we going to get those papers in the hands of all the voters in just one day?'

'We'll have to organize,' Stormy said thoughtfully.

Lowe shook his head. 'If we let a lot of

146

people in on the secret, Verdune will get word of it.'

'Nobody except just the four of us need know what we're printing in the paper,' Stormy explained. 'But we'll have to get an organization to get the papers distributed. You must have some man in your party who would know what people to choose in each community to get the papers spread around.'

Jim nodded. 'Ostrand.'

'He knows the big political wheels in every community,' Betty agreed. 'It was through him that we circulated the petition to get Jim's name on the ballot.'

'Get in touch with him,' Stormy ordered with the air of a commanding general. 'Have him alert men in every community. We'll get the papers to them a day or two before election. It will be their responsibility to see that every voter gets a paper.'

'Gramp will jump at the chance to go to McCook to see Mr. Ostrand,' Betty suggested.

Enthusiasm was high as the four started to leave the room for work at the printing office. But steps outside the door brought them up short. Stormy answered when a knock rattled the door. Fyfe flung the door open and came in, angry eyes flashing over the room.

'Claude sent me to bring you home,' he said flatly.

Stormy faced Fyfe defiantly. 'Then I'll send you back to tell him to go stiff-legged.'

Fyfe's normally fair skin darkened as anger poured into his face. 'Claude said to bring you and I figure he meant just that.' He clutched Stormy's arm. 'Come on.'

Stormy slapped him, a blow that landed so quickly Fyfe had no chance to dodge. The lawyer swore and grabbed Stormy with both hands, swinging her toward the door.

Jim leaped forward and clutched Fyfe's shoulder, fingers biting deep. 'She said for you to go. Can't you understand English?'

The lawyer flinched under Jim's pinching fingers. He released Stormy and took a quick swing, tagging Jim sharply on the jaw. The blow hurt, but satisfaction poured through Jim. Fyfe was giving him the chance he had been hoping for.

He backed off a step, and when Fyfe tried to follow, he snapped forward, cracking his knuckles on the lawyer's flabby face. Blood came through the broken skin and Fyfe reeled backward, cursing wildly.

Jim was not to be denied. Here was the brains behind Verdune's dirty work. And he could think of nothing right now but the stories that had been going the rounds, stories that dragged Stormy's name in the mud along with his own. Every blow he landed was easing the pressure built up by his anger.

Fyfe back-pedaled rapidly out of the room and to the top of the stairs. Then a vicious right from Jim caught him on the jaw and rocked him back into the stairway. He turned a backward somersault, landing on his face and sliding halfway down the steps. There he lodged.

Jim waited for Fyfe to get up, aware that Eddie Lowe was at his elbow although neither Betty nor Stormy had come out of the room. Fyfe looked up, then got slowly to his feet.

'I'll make you pay for this, Taylor,' he said thickly.

'There's no time like the present,' Jim said, and started down the steps.

But Fyfe wheeled and bounded down the stairs and out of the hotel ahead of Jim.

CHAPTER FOURTEEN

The polls opened amidst an uneasy calm. Eddie Lowe had closed his office and come down to the store at Jim's request. Betty and Stormy were there, too, but against Jim's wishes. From the window of the store they could watch the polling place just across the street in the town hall.

'We'd better get our voting done while we can,' Jim suggested to Lowe, and the two went across to the hall. After casting his ballot, Jim wandered among the early voters, watching the ballots as they were checked. Those at the polls now were homesteaders from down the creek, men who had been handed the special edition

149

of the paper late yesterday.

The settlers he had asked soon came across from the polling place to the store. They were heavily armed, and Stormy and Betty looked at them in surprise.

'Just a precaution,' Jim said lightly.

He was finding it hard to believe that one of the papers hadn't fallen into the hands of a Verdune man by now. When a racket came from the edge of town, he wheeled, expecting to see Verdune's riders charging in. But it was Gramp in his spring wagon. And there was excitement clearly stamped on his face as he tied his team and hurried into the store.

Jim didn't ask Gramp for an explanation. Down beyond the hotel Ross Harder had left the drug store and was coming slowly up the street. Jim didn't need to be told that a Verdune man had finally read a copy of the paper.

'Trouble,' Lowe said, pointing at Harder, and fear choked his voice.

'He doesn't look very happy,' Jim admitted, taking a gun belt from under the counter where he always kept it handy and buckling it around his middle.

'Got an extra gun, Jim?' Gramp asked, apparently forgetting the news that had had him so excited.

'Plenty,' Jim said. 'I've been looking for some fireworks. You'll find a dozen guns back at the end of that lower shelf. There are several boxes of shells, too.'

Harder had hesitated in front of the Verdune House. He seemed to be listening, and Jim turned to look down the empty street into the prairie. Gramp came back, loading a six-gun.

'Looks like you were fixing to fight a war,' he remarked. 'Where's that varmint now?'

Then Jim saw them, the entire Flying V Bar crew with Verdune at the head. They wheeled into the end of the street and pulled up. Probably Verdune was wondering where Jim would be waiting for him. For Jim didn't underestimate Verdune. The rancher would expect him to be ready.

Jim made a quick count of the riders. Fourteen. Noble was at Verdune's elbow and Steve Shane was back at the edge of the group. But he couldn't locate Fyfe. Even at this distance, Jim could see that they were armed to the teeth.

'I didn't think he'd do that,' Stormy breathed beside Jim. 'What will this do to his political career?'

'No more damage than those stories you wrote,' Jim said, watching Gramp bring up a rifle to go with his six-shooter.

'But what will he gain?' Stormy said, a mixture of fear and anger putting an edge on her voice.

'He probably hopes to gain what he knows he can't win at the polls,' Jim said, shifting to get a better view down the street.

Verdune had made up his mind. He motioned some of his men to one side of the street and took the rest the other way. Harder stepped back into the protection of the hotel veranda and shouted to Verdune:

'They're in the store.'

Verdune waved that he understood, and his men dismounted and ducked behind the buildings.

'Is he going to fight, Jim?' Betty asked incredulously. 'Can't you talk him out of it?'

'The time for talk is past,' Jim said. 'All he wants now is to get rid of me and drive out the homesteaders.'

Gramp dropped down on a stool by the counter and jerked off his boots. Jim took his attention off Verdune's men for a moment.

'What's the idea, Gramp?' he demanded. 'We've got a fight coming up.'

'That's exactly the idea,' Gramp said solemnly. 'In a scrap, a man never knows what might happen. And I don't intend to die with my boots on.'

The first shot came from the lumber yard, a shot that shattered the front window and thudded into some bolts of cloth on a shelf. Jim whirled to the girls.

'Get into the back room. Art,' he called to one of the homesteaders, 'you stay back there with them and watch against a sneak attack from the rear.'

The firing picked up rapidly. Jim realized the defenders of the store were going to have their hands full. The attackers were using all the cover they could find, and all their fire was centered on the one target, Jim's store. It seemed to Jim that it must be only a matter of time before a few lucky shots would so reduce the defenders that Verdune's outfit could take the store with a rush. He wished he had sent for the sheriff from Sagehorn. But on election day, the sheriff would have been extremely reluctant to leave the county seat unless Jim could have produced positive proof that there was going to be trouble.

Jim brought up several boxes of ammunition, wishing all the while that he had made the girls go back to the hotel. Gramp and the homesteaders beside Jim were pouring bullets at the lumber yard where Verdune's men were holed up. But Jim waited. After the first flurry died down, men would get reckless. Then bullets could count.

Jim got his chance quicker than he expected. One of the Flying V Bar punchers tried to run from the lumber yard to the back of the town hall just across from the store. Jim used his gun then, and the puncher didn't make it.

When another puncher tried to get to the hall, Jim recognized Verdune's strategy. From the hall, they could throw bullets directly into the store, picking their targets inside the building.

'Don't let them get across that open space,' Jim yelled, using his gun more freely now.

He heard a groan beside him and turned to see one of the homesteaders gripping an arm.

'Got it in the arm,' he said when Jim crawled to him. 'Ain't bad, but it looks like I'm out of it.'

Before Jim got back to his place another nester caught a bullet in the leg. He grimaced in pain but kept his gun in action. Another lucky shot or two from the Flying V Bar and the defense of the store would be in bad shape.

A yell from the homesteader in back of the store brought Jim around. He guessed that the men Verdune had sent down the alley were close enough to make trouble at the back of the store. Jim sent the unharmed nester back to help his partner while he and Gramp and Lowe continued to meet the attack from the front.

'We're going to get holes burned in our britches if this keeps up,' Gramp prophesied as he reloaded his gun. 'Art and Jed will have their hands full back there, and we ain't on a picnic up here. If a couple more of us gets plugged, they'll run right over what's left.'

The homesteader called Art came from the back room in a crouching run. He stopped by Jim, yelling to make himself heard above the shooting.

'One of those hyenas got through from the livery barn. He's standing right against the wall of the store. Ain't trying to break in yet, just keeping out of sight and yelling for you. Can't tell what he's saying most of the time, but he talks like he wants to side with us. You'd better go back and see. I'll take over here.'

Jim left his spot behind the boxes he had piled up and ran to the back of the store. It was some trick, he supposed. But if one of Verdune's men had made it across to the store, something had to be done. If left alone, he could set the store on fire.

Stormy, a gun in one hand, caught Jim's arm as he came through the partition door. 'It's Steve. He says he wants to throw in with us.'

Jim thought of his old partner and wondered.

'Are you sure it's Steve?'

Stormy nodded, and Jim wheeled to the back door. He slipped the lock and opened it a crack. 'Steve?'

'Here,' Steve said only inches away from the door. 'Let me in, Jim, and make it quick. I'm supposed to be firing the store. If they find out I'm double-crossing them, they'll plug me.'

Jim knew what he had to do. He opened the door suddenly, and Steve darted in. A hail of bullets riddled a panel of the door as Jim slammed it shut. The homesteader had his gun centered on Steve. Jim looked at his old partner, and his doubts faded.

'He's all right, Jed,' he said, and the settler turned back to the fighting. 'What's the idea, Steve?'

'I've had all of Verdune I can take.'

'It took you a while to get enough.'

Steve nodded. 'I know. That story he started about Stormy did it.'

Jim added his gun to the fight again. 'If you had come in a week ago, Steve, you could have helped us then.'

'I stayed with Verdune to find out what he was going to do. And I stayed almost too long. But I found out that he's planning to break into the town hall and stuff those ballot boxes.'

'He can't get away with it,' Betty cried.

'He can and he will if we don't stop him,' Steve said. 'If he licks you here, he'll be the big boss and nobody will dare say anything. When he gets the boxes stuffed and Fyfe gets the books worked over, he'll be elected.'

'Is Fyfe out there?' Jim asked.

Steve laughed. 'Fyfe turned white as a sheet when Verdune suggested he come along. He's waiting out of town. Verdune aims to burn you out of here, but if he can't lick you without a siege, he figures on stealing the ballot boxes and register books and taking them out to Fyfe.'

'We've got work to do,' Jim said, trying to think of a scheme to stop Verdune. He called through the partition door, 'Any of them made it across to the hall?'

'One just now,' Gramp yelled back in disgust. 'I got one trying to make it, but this ornery son came right when our guns were empty.'

Jim looked over the store. 'There's a window

156

on the north side. I can get out there. All of Verdune's outfit except Harder is to the south. I might be able to circle down past the Verdune House, cross the street, and work my way back.'

'Let's go,' Steve said. 'We're wasting time.'

'You want in this, too?'

'I wouldn't miss it. I'd like to meet up with Verdune with those ballot boxes.'

Jim turned toward the window, feeling better than he had for a long time. Having Steve beside him in this fight was a great morale builder. Crouching low to keep out of sight from the front, Jim led the way to the side window and jerked up the sash. Stormy, a gun in her hand, came after them.

'I'll cover you,' she said.

Jim smiled his thanks and slipped through the window. Both Stormy and Betty would be needed to defend the store now.

The Verdune House presented the first obstacle. They couldn't go to the front or the back, for Verdune's men would be able to see them either way.

'Have to go through windows again,' Jim said, and pushed up the first window he came to. Steve followed him through. They found themselves in an empty room. Crossing the hall carefully, they selected an empty room on the other side of the hotel. Jim controlled an urge to stop and rout out Harder. Time was too precious. Dropping out of the north window, they hurried on.

They went behind the drug store and the *Bugle* office, the back of the hotel reaching into the alley far enough to block them from sight of Verdune's men at the livery stable. Dropping over the bank of the creek, they waded through the rush grass close to the water's edge, climbing back up to the street level behind the blacksmith shop.

Here the town hall, being longer than the other buildings along this side of the street, reached back far enough to hide Jim and Steve from most of the lumber yard. Since all the Flying V Bar punchers at the lumber yard were concentrating on the store across the street anyway, Jim and Steve ran boldly up the alley. They passed the hardware and paused at the rear of Biggs' grocery to catch their breath.

Steve fingered his gun and glanced at Jim. Jim considered the open space between the store and the back door of the town hall, then looked at Steve.

'We've tackled worse things,' he said, and Steve nodded.

Jim went first, with Steve five feet behind. They had almost reached the door when a shout from the lumber yard ripped through the roar of battle and bullets began slapping the air around their ears.

Jim hit the door, and when Steve's weight crashed into him, the latch on the door gave way and they staggered inside. The men on the election board were crowded into a knot along the wall and two Flying V Bar men were holding them at gun point.

Jim dived to his left, bringing his gun around as he fell. Bullets tore splinters from the floor inches from his head, but his first shot knocked one man down. Before he could shoot again, Steve's gun roared and the other man spun around, letting his gun slip to the floor.

But a fresh outburst of shots from the store across the street warned Jim that help for the Flying V Bar men was coming from the lumber yard. He lunged to his feet and across the room toward a side window. There was a side door there, too, and before he got to the window that door flew open.

It was Bruce Noble, Verdune's foreman, who charged in. He bumped into Jim, knocking him backward. His eyes lit up as he brought his gun around. Jim, off balance, couldn't bring up his gun in time. He knew that death lay only a breath away.

But Steve yelled just then, and Noble whipped his gun around and fired. As Jim recovered his balance, he saw Steve reel backward. His yell had been only a decoy, not a battle cry, for he hadn't been ready, either.

Noble wheeled back, and the roar of his gun blended with Jim's. But Jim had his shot timed to the whirling body of the big foreman. Noble's bullet plowed into the floor as he crashed forward. Another man reeled into the door, but a bullet from across the street had

159

taken the fight out of him. Jim spun toward Steve.

'Just in the leg,' Steve said. 'Never mind me. See about the ballot boxes.'

'They're safe,' a grizzled official of the election board said. 'They were fixing to steal the whole works, books and all.'

The fighting outside suddenly died down. Jim ran to the window and looked out in time to see a half-dozen horsemen mounting up beyond the lumber yard. Verdune was licked in this battle.

He hurried into the street to meet the defenders from the store. Gramp, still minus his boots, fired a last shot at the horsemen, then broke into a hilarious jig.

But Jim, watching the departing riders with Verdune at their head, realized that the fight wasn't over. The ballots, perhaps the election, had been saved. But as long as Claude Verdune lived and controlled the Flying V Bar, there would be trouble for the homesteaders.

'Say,' Gramp said suddenly, stopping his jig. 'I almost forgot what I was hurrying into town for this morning. When I was in McCook before, I sent a letter to the sheriff of Green County in Kansas, asking about a man who was supposed to have killed Sam Harder.'

Eddie Lowe caught his breath, threw a frightened look at Jim, then turned to Gramp. 'How did you find out about that?'

'I nosed around in some things that were

160

none of my business, I guess,' Gramp said. 'It was while I was down at the printing office one day waiting for you, Eddie. I found out what Verdune had on you. I've been waiting for the answer to the letter I sent to that sheriff. I had it sent to Sand Creek because I didn't trust nobody in this town, not even the post-master. That letter came yesterday. They caught the real murderer, and Eddie ain't wanted any more.'

Jim watched the surprise and relief sweep over Lowe's face as Gramp went into the store.

A celebration might have been staged in the street then and there, but Jim cut it short with a low word of warning. Out on the veranda of the Verdune House, Ross Harder stood glaring down at them. Behind him was one of the Flying V Bar riders.

Jim guessed at a glance what had happened. Verdune had sent the rider around to Harder with the word that Lowe was the man he wanted for killing his brother. Now Harder was not to be stopped. Any hope that he had had for power and wealth had been dissipated with Verdune's defeat. Revenge was the only thing left for him. And that would be aimed at the man he thought had killed his brother.

Harder came slowly down the steps of the veranda, the Flying V Bar puncher, Jessel, beside him. 'Lowe,' he said sharply, 'get away from those women.'

Betty clutched Lowe's arm. 'You can't fight

161

him, Eddie.'

'I didn't suppose you were too good to shoot women, Ross,' Stormy said, looking contemptuously at the gunman.

Harder moved forward a couple of steps, his fists clenched. 'Maybe I ain't where you're concerned. Draw, Lowe. I'll show you what happens to a man that murders a Harder.'

'He didn't kill your brother,' Jim said sharply, moving up beside Lowe. 'They've caught the man who did.'

Harder laughed sneeringly. 'Are you trying to crawfish for him, Taylor? If they'd caught anybody, I'd have heard about it. I'm giving you a chance, Lowe. That's more than you gave Sam.'

Lowe turned to Betty, pushing gently. 'Get back out of the way. I've got to do this.'

Betty stood her ground. 'But you can't. You won't have a chance.'

'He's right, Betty,' Jim said softly. 'He can't avoid this and live like a man afterward.'

Betty turned on Jim. 'Are you backing out?'

Her words jarred him, and he realized suddenly what had been gnawing at him. This wasn't his fight. It was strictly between Lowe and Harder. The code of honor barred him from interfering. But he knew the odds against the editor. And it was a fight without good cause. He had to stand by Lowe.

'I'm not much good at backing up. Gramp,' he said to the old man just coming out of the

162

store, 'get the girls back.'

Growling at being left out of it, Gramp guided Stormy and Betty back to the front of the store. Harder scowled at Jim, still standing beside Lowe.

'You're not taking cards in this,' he said.

'I'm just making sure Jessel stays out,' Jim said gently. 'If there's anything left of you when Eddie gets through, you and I have a little business to settle.'

Harder was uncertain for the first time since leaving the hotel. 'Like what?' he demanded.

'I didn't take kindly to being tossed in Gramp's cellar,' Jim said. 'I figure you ought to apologize for that.'

'I'll apologize with a hot slug,' Harder grated.

'That suits me,' Jim said. 'Maybe right now would be a good time.'

It had worked even better than he had expected. The unwritten law of these people watching along the street demanded that each man fight his own batle. But now this fight was his as much as Lowe's.

Harder turned his attention back to Lowe, ignoring Jim, obviously realizing his mistake in letting himself be dragged into a quarrel with him.

Words were of no use now. Jim made a sudden move. Harder spun toward Jim, dragging at his gun.

Jim's hand flashed for his gun at the same

time Eddie moved. But Lowe wasn't in the race. All the speed Jim had acquired through the years came to his aid now. His .45 spoke a breath ahead of Harder's gun. Jim felt a slug burn across his ribs and he flinched, but he stood, feet wide spread, and squeezed the trigger twice more.

Harder stumbled forward, his gun held loosely in his hand, then spilled into the dust of the street. Jessel had started to draw, but the guns had roared before his gun cleared leather and he dropped it back, raising his hands. Lowe, too, had got his gun clear only after the tide of battle had turned.

'One less skunk to stink up the place,' Gramp said, breaking the silence that hung over the town after the guns had roared.

Lowe turned to Jim, white and shaken now. 'Thanks, Jim,' he said earnestly.

Jim shook his head. 'Don't thank me. That was a personal squabble Harder and I had to settle. It just wasn't your day.'

Jim turned away, met Betty's grateful eyes, and went on into the store. It wasn't the first time he had met a man over flaming guns. But he still couldn't quiet the pangs that always struck him when the smoke cleared.

But Verdune was on his mind now more than Harder. The rancher might leave the country, but Jim doubted it. He wouldn't be licked as long as he held a trump card. And Jim couldn't believe he had played his last trump today.

CHAPTER FIFTEEN

Jim had two good nurses to clean and bandage the wound in his side. Stormy and Betty made too much fuss, he thought, over a mere scratch.

Gramp came in once to report that the officials over in the town hall said Jim was leading Verdune five to one. That in the precinct where Verdune was supposed to own the voters body and soul.

But Gramp's enthusiasm about the election was nothing compared to the excitement that propelled him into the store a few minutes later.

'Hey, Jim,' he yelled. 'There's a prairie fire over west.'

Jim's lethargy vanished and he came out of the store on the run.

He looked at the smoke in the west and quickly took in the situation. There wasn't much breeze, but what there was struck him in the face as he stood with eyes fixed on that smoke.

'It's several miles away,' Jim said. 'Beyond your homesteads.'

Gramp nodded. 'And headed right for them. Somebody's trying to burn us out.'

Like a flash, Jim had the answer. Verdune! He was playing his last trump—fire. Steve Shane, limping on his wounded leg, hobbled up.

'Let's get out there and turn that fire,' he

shouted. 'Verdune said he'd never be licked by the homesteaders. I reckon he's trying to make good on that threat.'

Jim wheeled to Gramp, taking command. 'Get all the men and wagons you can. I've got some barrels. Get all the barrels that Biggs and Nichols have, too. Fill them with water from the creek. We may not be able to get enough water out there. Take what rags and sacks you can find.'

'Biggs may not let us have his barrels,' Steve said.

'We won't ask him,' Gramp shouted, running toward the grocery across the street. 'We'll just take them. Let's go.'

Jim hurried into the store and located his empty barrels. When Gramp brought a couple of homesteaders with wagons, Jim had four barrels and a big armload of sacks waiting on the porch.

Betty came running down the street from the drug store where she had been helping load a wagon. Jim called to her:

'Ride out to the homesteads and make sure Wes and the others are plowing fire guards west of all the buildings.'

Betty waved that she understood and raced for a horse. She disappeared down the street, and Jim turned to the wagons, following them to the dam where they filled the barrels.

'Where's Stormy?' Jim asked Steve as they mounted the nearest wagon and started rolling

166

up the street.

'She went out to the ranch about half an hour ago. Said she had left a lot of things there she wanted. She figured that Verdune wouldn't go back to the ranch for a while and, with all the hands gone, it would be a good time to clean out her stuff.'

Jim nodded and looked at the fire, reddening the sky now as it gained momentum. It was north of the Flying V Bar. She would be safer at the ranch than with the fire fighters. At the livery barn, Jim and Steve dropped off the wagon. Jim got his horse and Steve slapped a saddle on another one.

They pounded out of town, passing the water wagons a mile down the road. They arrived at Ward's homestead, directly in the path of the blaze, several minutes ahead of the wagons. Ward and the other homesteaders were out to the west plowing furrows through the prairie. A fifty-yard strip of grass was left between the furrows, and a match was touched to the grass inside these plowed barriers.

'Keep this backfire from jumping the furrows,' Jim yelled to the woman who had come out to help. The men raced on to plow more furrows between the fire and other homesteads. Until the wagons got there, the fighters soaked aprons, sacks, and even shirts in water pumped from Ward's well and beat at any spark that leaped the furrows. But they needed more rags and more water. Jim

167

watched anxiously for the wagons.

The first of the wagons arrived, and with it came men on horseback. Jim could scarcely believe his eyes when he saw Tom Biggs, bareheaded, jolting along on the second wagon. Jim leaped into a wagon, grabbed some of the sacks he had put there, and began dousing them in the water barrels and handing them to the men, women, and children who were waiting.

The head fire was gaining speed. The sun had disappeared behind a pall of smoke and the air was hot and stifling. Gramp had taken command of one of the wagons, directing it to the northwest where men with soaked rags and sacks beat at the edge of the blaze to keep it from spreading. Steve Shane took another wagon and did the same on the south flank. The fire was cutting a path a quarter of a mile wide now, and three homesteads were directly in its course.

Jim helped the fighters hold the backfire in bounds. It soon burned all the grass between the plowed furrows, and the big threat that remained was that sparks from the main fire bearing down on them might leap the burned strip.

Jim found himself beside Tom Biggs, who was perspiring in the stifling heat until he looked as if he had been ducked in a water barrel.

'What are you doing out here?' Jim

168

demanded.

'Same thing you are,' Biggs panted. 'This fire will go right on to town if we don't stop it.'

'Maybe that's what Verdune wants. I figure he started it.'

Biggs looked at Jim and nodded. 'Maybe. He's bossed me around a lot and I took it. But he ain't going to burn me out without a fight.'

Jim turned away. Revenge was all that Verdune would get out of this day's work. His grip on the upper end of Buffalo Creek was broken.

Soaking his sack again, Jim mounted his horse, making a quick estimate of the progress of the fire. It was coming faster now. They wouldn't be able to stop the head fire. All they could hope to do would be divert it and save the buildings, keeping it boxed into as narrow a strip as possible. They would need help on the flanks to do that. There were enough fighters left here to save the buildings. The crops that were still in the fields would be lost.

Jim reached the southern flank where a shift in the breeze seemed to be crowding the fire over in spite of efforts to stop it. Steve Shane was limping around, working feverishly, face glowing from the heat.

'We can't hold it,' he yelled as Jim dismounted and tied his horse to the back end-gate of the wagon. 'The wind seems to be changing. And it's getting higher.'

Jim pitched in with the fighters flaying at the

169

edges of the blaze. Uneasiness prodded him. A fire always created air disturbances that usually caused a wind. If the wind came up with this fire blazing as it was now, it would run wild.

'Tell all the men to stay close to the wagons and their horses,' Jim yelled. 'We may have to get out in a hurry.'

For the next few minutes, Jim fought the licking flames. Then suddenly Steve yelled almost in his ear:

'The wind has changed to the north.'

Jim stopped and moved back from the heat. The head fire was dying down like a bonfire without fuel. But behind them to the west, smoldering embers that had not been completely beaten out were being fanned into new life by the wind, starting a hundred little blazes that merged into one and began eating into the prairie to the south.

'That will be a good one on Verdune,' one settler panted. 'That's heading straight for his layout now. And I ain't going to fight to turn it away from him.'

Jim caught his breath, realizing that the homesteader had analyzed the situation accurately. The fire, gaining speed like a heavy freight train, was aiming directly at the Flying V Bar. And Stormy was there. Jim wheeled toward his horse tied to the wagon

'Where are you going, Jim?' Steve demanded.

'Stormy's at the ranch,' he called back,

swinging into the saddle.

'You'd better hurry,' Steve yelled. 'The wind is coming up fast.'

Jim needed no urging. The wind was rising higher every second, and the fire to the west was leaping as it roared forward. Tumbleweeds caught in the flame were hurled forward by the wind to land and start fresh blazes. Jim saw smoldering buffalo chips, set afire in the original blaze, picked off the blackened area and rolled out into the dry grass to the south, leaving trails of new fire as they went.

He came to Buffalo Creek, no wider than ten feet, and splashed across it. The creek might prove a barrier to a small fire that wasn't being driven by a high wind. But it wouldn't hold up this blaze for an instant.

Across the creek, Jim reined his horse to the west along the bank of the stream. Here the smoke crowded in on him and he had to fight his horse to keep him on the course. Cattle splashed across the creek and raced into the south; blind, fear-crazed animals that threatened to run over him.

When the cattle were past, Jim urged his horse on, fighting his head with a strong rein. Smoke swirled down in clouds, almost choking him at times. The air was getting hot and sweat soaked his shirt.

He had just caught sight of the ranch buildings through veils of smoke when a horse pounded out of the yard, reins flying. Jim dug

171

in his spurs. That was Stormy's horse. She was afoot now in the path of that roaring inferno. He raced into the yard, looking frantically for the girl. But smoke curled down over the house and blotted out the buildings.

He called loudly as he dismounted. He heard an answer and pulled his nervous horse toward the sound. The smoke was lifted suddenly by a gust of wind, and he saw her. But he stopped short as if a bullet had struck him. Claude Verdune had one arm wrapped tightly around the girl, and in his other hand was a gun.

'I'll take that horse,' Verdune yelled, and propelled Stormy toward Jim.

Jim fought down his surprise. Evidently Verdune had come back to the ranch and his horse had gotten away from him, too. Now he saw his chance to get a horse, and he was using Stormy for a shield.

'We might all ride one horse,' Jim suggested.

Verdune laughed wildly as he pushed Stormy ahead. 'Only one of us goes. No horse can outrun that fire carrying double.'

'Surely you'll take Stormy?'

Verdune was within five feet of Jim now. 'I ain't taking nobody. Give me that horse.'

Jim considered his chances. He couldn't use a gun, not with Verdune holding Stormy as a shield. On the other hand, Verdune dared not shoot him, for if Jim let go of the reins, the horse would bolt and no one would leave the

172

ranch yard ahead of the fire. Verdune would have to come to Jim to get the horse.

'Give me the reins,' Verdune ordered, stopping three feet from Jim.

Jim held out the reins, then suddenly shoved them into Stormy's hand. His eyes whipped to Verdune's face just as the rancher rocked back from a shove of Stormy's elbow.

The gun roared, but the bullet went wild as Jim shot a hand out to grasp Verdune's wrist. Verdune was still staggering back when Jim twisted his gun free. It fell in the dust, and Jim gave the rancher no chance to reach for it.

'Get out of here,' he yelled to Stormy as he drove a fist deep into Verdune's flabby stomach.

But he knew she wouldn't go and leave him.

Verdune fought like the madman he was. Head down, he charged like a bull. Jim beat at Verdune's head, but he couldn't find a vulnerable spot and he was shoved back. His legs hit the edge of the low watering trough and he toppled backward into it.

With a yell of triumph, Verdune grabbed a stub post leaning against the windmill tower and swung it at Jim's head as he came up out of the water. Jim saw the blow coming and ducked under the rim of the trough, and the post splintered in Verdune's hand as it struck the tank. Jim vaulted out of the trough and came back at Verdune, who dropped the splintered post and rushed to meet him.

173

The impromptu bath had cooled Jim, and he met Verdune's charge with renewed strength. This time the rancher's madman strength didn't prevail. Inch by inch Jim drove him back, trying desperately for a crippling punch. Verdune began to weaken.

A scream from Stormy jerked Jim's attention away for a second. His heart seemed to sink to his toes as he saw the horse dragging the girl across the yard. Fear had seized the animal as the fire swept closer, and Stormy dragging on the reins only increased his panic.

Verdune had stopped to watch the girl, too, and when she lost her grip on the reins and the horse bolted to the south, Verdune wheeled with a hysterical scream and raced after the animal.

Jim watched him go, his mind searching for some means of escape from the flaming death roaring in from the north. The course Verdune had chosen wasn't the way. No man on foot could outrun that fire. It would take the best of horses to do it. And there were no horses there now.

Jim ran across the yard to Stormy. 'Are you hurt?' he asked as she got to her feet.

'No,' she said, tears were streaming down her face. 'But that horse was our only hope. We'll be burned alive.'

Jim looked over the smoke-filled yard, recalling the sweep of prairie to the south of the buildings. 'We've got a chance,' he said grimly. 'You get some sacks, soak them in the watering trough and bring them to me. I'll be south of the barn.'

He didn't wait for her answer but ran around the barn. The smoke was swirling down in smothering clouds and the heat was drying his skin to cracklings. He found the grass south of the corral tinder dry and almost hot enough to burst into flame. Taking a match from his pocket, he struck it and tossed it into the grass. By the time Stormy came with the water-soaked sacks, the blaze was leaping high and heading south with the wind.

'Why did you do that?' Stormy gasped, coughing in the smoke. 'Isn't it bad enough to have fire on one side?'

'Being between two fires is better than being in the middle of one,' he said, trying to sound confident.

The head fire was across the creek now and licking up the slope to the buildings. Even as they watched, the roof of the house erupted in flame.

'The barn will go next and we'll be roasted,' Stormy said, her endurance almost gone.

'Wrap these wet sacks around your feet,' Jim said.

Time had run out. The smoldering grass ahead was not cool enough to walk on, but they couldn't wait. He helped Stormy wrap sacks on her feet, then wound some on his own.

Taking the girl's arm, he moved out on the

175

burned area, following close behind the fire he had started, which was not making much headway yet. The heat rising from the ground and whirling in on them from the main fire behind burned their lungs and robbed them of breath. Smoke blinded them, and when Stormy stumbled, Jim was tested to the utmost to keep her from falling in the hot smoldering grass.

Finally Jim called a halt. 'We'll wait it out here,' he choked. 'If we're not safe now, we can't make it.'

They stood close together, blinded and almost suffocated by the smoke and heat.

Time dragged on, and gradually the smoke thinned enough so that Jim could see where the main body of the fire had split, racing along on either side of the area burned over by the little fire he had set.

The air cleared and the heat began to lessen. Jim grinned through dry cracked lips. 'We made it, Stormy,' he said hoarsely.

There was a sob in Stormy's voice as she looked over the burned prairie and the blazing ruins of the Flying V Bar buildings. 'I didn't think anything could be so horrible.'

'Can you walk?' he asked.

She nodded, but winced when she took a step to prove it. Jim knew how she felt. His feet were burned and his skin was as dry as paper.

'Let's go up to the creek,' he suggested. 'It won't be so hot there.'

They reached the creek and found some

rush grass that had been too wet to burn. That wet grass was like a velvet carpet.

They were still sitting there when Gramp came along an hour later with a wagon. He was humped over on the seat looking at the blackened ashes of the Flying V Bar, still hot and smoldering. Only the walls of the sod half of the barn and the bunkhouse were still standing. Jim got to his feet when he heard the rattle of the wagon. Gramp saw him, and the whoop he sent out into the cooling air reverberated along the creek.

'I was looking for the charred remains,' he said, pulling the wagon to a halt just above the two. 'I don't know how you pulled through, but, by Henry, you did it and that's all that matters. I'll help you in and we'll get back to town.

* * *

The Bluestem *Bugle* was a day late that week getting into the post office. Its editor was helping Gramp and Betty in their nursing chore down at Jim's store.

Jim only vaguely remembered those first painful days. But he was sitting up in bed when Eddie came in after mailing his weekly papers.

'You're looking better,' Lowe said, crossing to the bed. 'I just put my paper in the mail. There are only two stories in it this week. One tells of your six to one sweeping victory over Verdune, and the other is about a big prairie

177

fire and the end of a range hog.'

Jim glanced at Stormy standing by the side window. 'That wasn't a pretty ending even for a range hog,' he said.

'Claude started that fire,' Stormy said, moving away from the window. 'He told me so. He wanted to burn out the homesteaders.'

Jim looked through the window at the sun shining on the side of the hotel that bore Verdune's name. 'He burned the prairie and the prairie took its vengeance.'

Stormy, who had less severe burns than Jim, came over to sit on the edge of his bed. Betty came in from the front of the store and called to Eddie.

'You're needed up here, Eddie.'

Lowe looked around, puzzled. 'I am?'

'Well, you're certainly not needed there.'

Lowe grinned foolishly, then hurried toward the partition door. 'I guess my eyes are getting bad.'

'What am I going to do with my store now?' Jim said thoughtfully.

'I think Gramp would make a good storekeeper while you're in Lincoln, don't you? And there will be a lot of business for a store now. Homesteaders will pour in. That's the way it should be.'

'They can thank you for that,' he said, taking her hand. 'I've just been thinking, Stormy. I don't know much about politics. I'm going to need an advisor when I get to Lincoln. Any

178

applications?'

She smiled. 'Just one, I hope. But it's not politics that I'm interested in. It's the politician.'

He reached an arm around her. 'I thought I'd run onto a wild little ruffian that first night down along the creek. I certainly made a mistake.'

She leaned against him. 'Maybe you're making a mistake now.'

He shook his head. 'I'm sure now. How about you?'

'I've been sure for a long time, Jim.'

Gramp came through the partition door. 'Say, Jim, I—' He broke off and spun back toward the front of the store. 'It sure is a pretty day, ain't it?' he murmured, closing the door behind him.